PUFFIN BO

The Lightning Sting

Dan Lee spends his time travelling between Asia and Britain. A wing chun master, he also trains in kickboxing and ju-jitsu.

Books in The Tangshan Tigers series

TANGSHAN TIGERS

The Lightning Sting

Dan Lee

PUFFIN

With special thanks to Brandon Robshaw

PUFFIN BOOKS

Published by the Penguin Group
Penguin Books Ltd, 80 Strand, London WC2R ORL, England
Penguin Group (USA) Inc., 375 Hudson Street, New York, New York 10014, USA
Penguin Group (Canada), 90 Eglinton Avenue East, Suite 700, Toronto, Ontario, Canada M4P 2Y3
(a division of Pearson Penguin Canada Inc.)
Penguin Ireland, 25 St Stephen's Green, Dublin 2, Ireland (a division of Penguin Books Ltd)
Penguin Group (Australia), 250 Camberwell Road, Camberwell, Victoria 3124, Australia
(a division of Pearson Australia Group Pty Ltd)
Penguin Books India Pvt Ltd, 11 Community Centre, Panchsheel Park, New Delhi – 110 017, India
Penguin Group (NZ), 67 Apollo Drive, Rosedale, North Shore 0632, New Zealand
(a division of Pearson New Zealand Ltd)
Penguin Books (South Africa) (Pty) Ltd, 24 Sturdee Avenue, Rosebank,
Johannesburg 2196, South Africa

Penguin Books Ltd, Registered Offices: 80 Strand, London WC2R ORL, England

puffinbooks.com

First published 2008
1

Series created by Working Partners Ltd, London
Text copyright © Working Partners Ltd, 2008
All rights reserved

The moral right of the author has been asserted

Set in Bembo
Typeset by Palimpsest Book Production Limited, Grangemouth, Stirlingshire
Made and printed in England by Clays Ltd, St Ives plc

British Library Cataloguing in Publication Data
A CIP catalogue record for this book is available from the British Library

ISBN: 978-0-141-32488-3

www.greenpenguin.co.uk

Penguin Books is committed to a sustainable future
for our business, our readers and our planet.
The book in your hands is made from paper
certified by the Forest Stewardship Council.

CONTENTS

THE RETURN OF CHANG

'And so I would like you all to welcome back our respected martial arts master and coach . . . Chang Sifu!' said Mr Wu, the principal.

Matt clapped as hard as he could. Every student in the huge Assembly Hall, with its light-sensitive, colour-changing mosaic walls, was applauding. But no one was applauding as loudly as Matt and his friends the Tangshan Tigers – Shawn, Catarina and Olivier.

The Tigers were a secret crime-fighting gang that Matt had formed with his best friends from the martial arts squad in his first term at the Beijing International Academy.

Matt's hands were soon stinging. Even though he had lost his own place on the martial arts squad, he was still really happy to see Chang back in the school.

Master Chang walked modestly on to the stage, his head bowed. Mr Wu waved the audience on to applaud even more, like a ringmaster at a circus.

The only person who didn't seem glad to welcome Chang back was Carl Warrick.

'It's a drag Sensei Ryan's gone,' he muttered from his place beside Matt. 'He knew what he was doing, that guy.'

'Sure,' said Olivier dryly. 'That would be why he's sitting in a police cell right now, waiting to be deported.'

The Tangshan Tigers laughed. Carl turned away crossly, his face reddening.

Mr Wu had milked the applause as long as he decently could. He walked to the front of the stage and made calming motions with his hands. The light twinkled off his cufflinks and glittering steel spectacles.

'As you know, I always have the best interests of this school at heart. I knew that Chang was the best man for the job – and Master Chang agrees with me!'

Matt rolled his eyes. It was thanks to Mr Wu that Chang had left in the first place. Not only that, it was the Tangshan Tigers who'd had to prove that Chang's replacement, Sensei Ryan, was secretly employed by a criminal named Sang. Sang had paid Ryan to ruin Chang's reputation. Needless to say, Chang had won *that* fight. Chang was a true master of martial arts.

'He's such a hypocrite!' Matt said out of the corner of his mouth to the Tigers.

Catarina grinned and Shawn winked at him.

'Don't worry about it, Matt,' said Catarina.

'It's pretty funny when you think about it,' said Olivier.

'We know who got Chang his job back,' said Shawn. 'That's all that matters.'

'I guess you're right,' said Matt, feeling cheered again.

'And now,' said Mr Wu, 'I'd like to ask Chang Sifu to say a few words. Come forward, my friend; yes, that's right – stand just here, next to me.' He placed his hand on Chang's shoulder. 'Pray silence for Chang Sifu.'

The two men formed a strange contrast, thought Matt as he sat back down. Mr Wu was so smart and dapper in his well-cut black suit, standing stiffly and proudly. Beside him stood the slightly taller figure of Chang in his martial arts attire: relaxed, calm, arms hanging by his side. *Chang looks so much more impressive*, Matt thought.

Chang Sifu coughed politely. 'Thank you very much for warm welcome. It means much to me. I am glad to be back. Beijing Academy team has match coming up in two weeks and I must prepare squad. After assembly, could the following students report to the *kwoon*: Catarina Ribeiro, Shawn Hung, Olivier Girard, Carl Warrick, Lola Adebayo, Paolo Zapata, Wolfgang Becker, Abdul Halwani, Andrei Drago, Jahmal Dangerfield . . . and Matt James.'

Matt's heart thudded inside his chest at the sound of his name. He was back in the squad! Matt had suffered an injury after Sensei Ryan had forced him to train too hard, and he'd been dropped to make way for the new boy, Andrei Drago.

The Tangshan Tigers cheered.

'Yay!' said Catarina.

'Way to go, Matt!' said Shawn.

'We said you'd get back in the team!' Olivier added.

Matt smiled. He was too happy to speak.

'So, you've squeezed your way back in somehow, have you?' sneered Carl. 'I might have guessed. Teacher's pet!'

'Matt is not a teacher's pet,' said Catarina. 'He's a great fighter and you know it!'

'All right, all right,' said Matt, embarrassed. 'Let Carl think what he likes, I don't care.'

The rest of the team made it clear they weren't with Carl on this one.

'Welcome back, Matt!' said Lola.

'Yeah, it's good to have you with us again,' said Wolfgang.

Even Andrei Drago gave Matt a faint grin.

The squad was standing outside the *kwoon*,

waiting for Master Chang to open the doors. Through the glass they could see the spacious, high-ceilinged hall. There was a white square of matting for combat in the middle, scarlet dragons painted on the wall, and Chang Sifu himself kneeling at the far end, head bowed in meditation as usual before a training session.

'Look at him!' said Carl impatiently. 'Why does he waste his time on that rubbish? The guy should be running a monastery, not a martial arts team! I'd hoped he'd have shaped up while he was away, but it doesn't look like it. The guy's past it, that's what I reckon.'

Matt wasn't prepared to hear him criticize Chang. 'Yeah?' he said. 'Well, I think Master Chang is a great coach and so does everyone else! It was thanks to him we won the last two tournaments —'

'It was thanks to *me* we won the last one!'

Carl interrupted. 'If I hadn't won my bout –'

'Civilization would have crumbled,' said Olivier, in his pitch-perfect imitation of Carl's voice. 'Without me, the great Carl Warrick, human life would grind to a halt!'

Carl glared at him. The rest of the squad burst out laughing.

Master Chang had risen now and Matt saw him striding towards the door.

'Come in, team. Ready for session of hard work today, I hope. Welcome, Matt. Vincent Poirier has had to return to France, so space available for you. You would not have been dropped anyway, I'm sure, but for injury.'

'It's great to be back!' said Matt.

Carl made sick noises in his throat.

'Are you unwell, Carl?' asked Chang.

Carl shook his head sulkily.

'Then let us begin. Please to form two lines,' Chang instructed the squad. 'I have announcement to make.'

Matt watched expectantly, wondering what the announcement could be. He glanced at the other Tigers. They looked as intrigued as he felt. As usual Chang's face was impassive, giving no clue as to whether the announcement was good or bad news.

When the squad had settled into two lines, Chang said: 'We are to take part in another tournament. Against very good team – the elite squad of Kensington International Academy.'

A murmur of excitement ran round the squad.

Matt felt his heartbeat quicken.

'Wow!' he murmured.

'What?' said Catarina, who was standing next to him.

'I know that school.'

It was only because his mother had been

posted to Beijing that Matt hadn't ended up at Kensington International Academy. It was the best known, most prestigious international school in London, and its martial arts team had an awesome reputation. They competed against all the top junior teams and hadn't lost a tournament for a long time.

'I nearly went there!' he told Catarina.

'Yeah?'

'Yeah, and some of my old friends from London are pupils there. I wonder if Harry's made the team? It'd be weird if I was competing against him –'

Chang Sifu glanced in Matt's direction and raised an eyebrow. Matt stopped talking.

'We will need a captain, of course. Catarina did very good job at tournament in Kyoto, but it is time for new captain. Who shall we choose? We need someone who does not chatter at wrong moment.' He looked meaningfully at Matt.

'On the other hand,' went on Chang, 'this is first time BIA squad will travel outside Asia for tournament – it will be best to choose someone who knows country and culture. That person will be Matt.'

'Oh, yesss!' said Matt, punching the air in jubilation. He'd gone from non-team member to captain in one morning – pretty good going! Catarina let out a whoop and Olivier clapped Matt on the back delightedly.

'Yay!' said Shawn. 'Go, Matt!'

'Wait a minute!' protested Carl. 'How come he just strolls back into the team and suddenly he's captain? Last time there was a test –'

'London is Matt's home,' said Chang calmly. 'This makes him most suitable captain for tournament in that city. If ever we have tournament against Sydney Institute of Excellence, you will be nominated captain, Carl. That is fair – yes?'

Carl nodded slowly. Matt noticed he still didn't look happy. But what was new? Carl hardly ever looked happy, unless he'd just got one up on somebody.

'And now,' said Chang, 'I have some bad news.' He looked grave. 'Very bad news indeed.'

'What do you think it is?' whispered Catarina.

'Dunno,' mouthed Matt.

'Because we fly to London tomorrow,' said Chang, 'we must spend all of today training and preparing. Very sorry to say this means all of today's lessons are cancelled for you.'

'Hooray!' shouted Catarina.

'Great!' said Olivier.

'Awesome!' added Shawn.

Everyone was cheering and whooping. Even Carl was smiling and shaking his head.

It was funny, thought Matt, laughing along with the rest of the team. Chang did not usually play jokes on them like this. *He must be as pleased to be back as I am!*

The noise subsided as Chang Sifu held up his hand for silence.

'Time to be serious,' he said. 'Today I teach you something important. It is a little trickier than last lesson I taught you – centre line theory, you remember?'

There were nods and murmurs of assent around the *kwoon*.

'Let me make check before we move on,' said Chang. 'Matt, tell us what centre line theory is.'

Matt paused for a moment to get his thoughts in order. 'It's a technique you can use with any martial arts discipline. You have

to face your opponent, and have all your
body – shoulders, hips, knees – pointing in
the same direction. When you strike, you
strike straight at an imaginary line in front of
you, running through the opponent's body.
No roundhouse kicks or punches –
everything moves along the most direct lines
of attack and defence.'

Chang nodded. 'Show.'

Matt went into the stance, his legs a
shoulder's width apart, weight resting on his
back foot. He threw a few straight punches
and mimed stiff blocks – all running along
the imaginary line in front of him.

'Good. Everyone.'

There was the sound of feet shuffling on
the mat as the rest of the squad assumed the
stance. Master Chang walked round,
checking, nodding approval, occasionally
pausing to adjust a knee or an elbow.

'Good,' said Chang again. 'A lesson well learned. Now to move on to subject of today's lesson. I am going to teach you *Chi Sao* game. Does anyone know of this?'

Matt looked at Shawn, who knew a lot about martial arts theory. He was a judo practitioner, and his grandfather was a kung fu exponent. But Shawn shrugged – even he didn't know about *Chi Sao*.

'Very well,' said Chang. '*Chi Sao* is a training drill. Principal aim: to improve sensitivity, makes one better able to anticipate attacks. If you play this game regularly your anticipation will improve so that you expect attack almost before it is made.'

Carl put up his hand. 'Hey, what's wrong with just using our good old-fashioned reflexes? If you've got good reflexes – like me – you'll always be able to react to an attack in time. And reflexes get better the

more you use them, everyone knows that,
so −'

'It is true you have good reflexes, Carl,'
said Chang mildly. 'But are they fast enough?
Let us test them. Come forward.'

Carl strode forward confidently.

'Take this coin,' said Chang. He dropped a
small gleaming silver coin into Carl's
outstretched palm. The rest of the team
crowded round to watch. 'Keep hand flat, like
so, yes. In a moment I shall pluck coin from
your hand − but you must try to close hand
before I can do so. Understand?'

'Yeah,' said Carl. 'Easy.'

'You are ready?'

'Sure −' began Carl, but before the word
had finished leaving his mouth, Chang's hand
had flicked out and removed the coin. Chang
held it up between finger and thumb.

Carl's face flushed a dull red. 'That wasn't

fair! I wasn't ready, you did it while I was
still speaking!'

'Then let us try again.'

He dropped the coin back into Carl's hand.
Carl tensed, eyes fixed on Chang. Matt could
see he was on the alert for the slightest
movement.

Again, Chang's hand swept out. Again,
Carl's hand closed on empty air. Again,
Chang held up the coin for everyone to see.

Matt couldn't help smiling. A few of the
squad giggled. Carl's boasting hadn't been
entirely false – it was true, he did have good
reflexes – but Chang was far too quick for him.

'OK, OK,' said Carl loudly. 'I'm not used
to this game, but I reckon I've got the hang
of it now. Gimme one more chance and I
bet you won't beat me this time!'

'Very well.' Matt saw a faint smile flit
across Chang Sifu's face.

Once more, Carl held out his hand with the coin in it. Chang's hand shot forward. It happened almost too fast for Matt to follow – there was a blur of motion, Carl's hand closed tight, and then Carl raised his fist in triumph.

'Yes! I did it!'

He danced round the motionless Chang, punching the air.

'I did it! That's what reflexes can do, right?'

'Show the class the coin, Carl,' said Chang Sifu quietly.

'What? Oh, sure.'

He held up the coin.

Matt gasped.

Then the rest of the class gasped as they saw what Matt had already noticed. The coin in Carl's hand wasn't silver.

It was copper.

Chapter 2

THE POWER OF *CHI SAO*

'Did you see that?' said Shawn. 'He switched coins –'

The grin faded from Carl's face as he realized what had happened. He stared at the copper coin in bewilderment.

'Is this what you are looking for?' asked Chang. He opened his hand to display the silver coin. 'You may return to your place, Carl.'

Scowling, Carl fell into line once more.

Chang walked in front of the semicircle of

students, making eye contact with each in turn. 'Purpose of this demonstration is to show that reflexes are not enough. Before Carl's fingers can close there is process of many stages. His eyes have to see slight movement on my part, then a message has to be sent to brain, then brain must send a message via nervous system to muscles that control fingers . . .' Chang lightly touched his own eyes, head, arm and fingers as he spoke to show the stages.

'This takes only fraction of a second – but fraction of second is long enough for me to do what I had always planned to do: snatch coin. This is trivial example, but principle applies in many situations – using brain can slow movement down.

'*Chi Sao* – which means 'Sticking Hands' – is a way of bypassing brain. We skip thinking and work entirely on instinct –

on touch.' Chang reached and lightly touched Matt on the shoulder. 'Master *Chi Sao* and you will not need to watch and think about what opponent is doing, and then react. You can defend yourself with much greater speed – and precision – because you will *feel* what opponent is about to do. Reaction immediate, not delayed.'

Matt wrinkled his brow. It sounded great – almost like a super-power. But how did it work? He didn't understand how you could 'feel' what someone was about to do. But he looked forward to learning.

'Get into pairs, please,' said Chang.

Matt found himself paired with Shawn. They grinned at each other.

'What do you think the drill's gonna be?' whispered Shawn.

'No idea,' said Matt. 'But if it's anything

like Chang's usual drills it's bound to be full of surprises!'

'Face each other. Now each put arms out, like so. Forearms should be touching – yes, both arms – contact should be firm but do not press hard.'

Matt placed his forearm against Shawn's. Their arms were cocked at a forty-five degree angle to their bodies as Chang had demonstrated.

'Now, roll hands from side to side – like so.' Chang illustrated the movement – a deft roll of the wrists. 'Maintain contact at all times – forearms must not separate. Be aware of feel of movement of partner's arm. Do not think about it, just feel it.'

Most students, Matt saw, felt a little self-conscious at first. They grinned at each other awkwardly as they rubbed forearms; Lola had a fit of the giggles, and Carl, who was paired with Andrei, kept muttering about how stupid it was. But after only a few repetitions everyone had settled into the routine. Silence fell. All around, Matt saw serious faces.

He had already fallen into a rhythm with Shawn. As he felt Shawn's wrists rolling, he rolled his own wrists in the same direction, constantly adjusting the angle and pressure of contact. He soon found he did not need to think about what movement Shawn would perform next – as he felt Shawn's muscles move against his, he just *knew* what to expect. Or rather, his arm knew.

This went on for a few minutes. When everyone was moving comfortably and rhythmically, Chang called out: 'All students who face me – when you are ready, you will launch attack on opponent. Hand strikes only. Until then, maintain contact. When you are ready, strike!'

23

Shawn was facing Chang. Matt braced himself for an attack. Meanwhile, his own and Shawn's arms kept moving, rolling, turning. Out of the corner of his eye, Matt saw one or two other students launching their attacks, but he took no notice, focusing all his attention on Shawn. A tense thirty seconds passed, Matt staring into Shawn's eyes, waiting for him to strike.

Suddenly Shawn made his move.

With his right arm, he swiftly thrust Matt's left arm to one side. Simultaneously he aimed a left-handed chop at Matt's neck. The strike was fast, accurate and delivered without any warning – but without Matt even thinking about it his right arm shot up and intercepted the strike in a perfect block.

Matt turned and looked at Chang, his mouth open in amazement. 'That was fantastic! My arm moved on its own, like it was on puppet strings or something. I didn't choose to block, I just did – like my arm *knew . . .*'

Chang Sifu gave one of his rare smiles. 'Yes, Matt. And this is the technique of *Chi Sao.*'

Chang kept the squad working on *Chi Sao* for the rest of the day, apart from a short break for lunch, followed by a period of rest and meditation. Then *Chi Sao* training was resumed. By the late afternoon, Matt had been paired with nearly all the other students in turn.

'This is great, isn't it?' he said to Olivier, after he'd just blocked a strike from him without even looking.

'Amazing,' Olivier agreed. 'I love the way you can feel yourself getting better at it – like you're discovering powers you had all along, but never knew.'

'Yeah, it's as if you can feel the little shift in energy that goes before a move,' said Matt, 'and you're not responding to it *after* it happens, but at the same time!'

Chang Sifu clapped his hands.

'Change partners, please. Find someone you have not yet worked with.'

The only student Matt hadn't paired up with was Carl. They faced each other and touched forearms. Matt looked into Carl's face, expecting to see the usual sneer there, or for Carl to make some sarcastic remark. But to his surprise Carl appeared to be taking the exercise seriously. He wore an expression of concentration. Unusually for Carl, he didn't say a word.

For a few seconds they rolled forearms together, settling into a rhythm. Hoping to catch Carl by surprise, Matt went for an early attack – a straight, super-fast spear-hand thrust, aimed directly at Carl's centre line. Instantly Carl blocked, pushing Matt's arm aside.

Matt felt a twinge of annoyance at having one of his best strikes blocked so easily. But he gave credit where it was due.

'Nice,' he said.

'Thanks.'

'It works, doesn't it, this *Chi Sao*?'

'I guess,' said Carl shortly.

'So it's been a pretty good session, hasn't it?' Matt couldn't resist teasing Carl a little after he'd been so scathing about Chang Sifu's training sessions.

'Well, I've been to worse,' said Carl, as though he was a professional inspector of martial arts lessons. 'It hasn't been completely useless.'

'So Chang's not past it then?'

'Maybe not completely,' said Carl grudgingly, as he turned away.

After they'd showered and changed it was time for supper. Matt and the Tigers sat together, chatting about the trip to London.

'What's the food like there?' asked Shawn. 'I heard it's not great.'

'No, English food is good!' said Matt. 'Roast beef, fish and chips, apple crumble – you'll love it. Anyway, London's such an international city, you can get any kind of food there. Chinese, Indian, French . . .'

'That's true,' said Olivier. 'There are so many good restaurants in London. I've been to some of them with my parents.' Olivier's mum and dad had worked all over the world as diplomats.

'Brazilian?' asked Catarina.

'Sure – anything!'

'It's a real happening city, isn't it?' asked Shawn.

'Yep. You can watch the best football in the world there – that's soccer to you, Shawn. There are always shows and exhibitions going on, and there are things like the London Eye – that's this massive big wheel by the side of the Thames, and you can go right up and you get such a fantastic view –'

'Sounds awesome,' said Catarina.

'Reckon we'll win the tournament?' asked Shawn. 'That *Chi Sao* training's gotta help.'

'They're a tough team, Kensington,' said Matt. 'Haven't lost for a long time.'

As he spoke, he realized that he'd have to meet Adam Bates again, and felt his first twinge of nerves. He was looking forward to seeing most of his old friends, but Adam had not been a friend. More like a bully throwing his weight around. He was seriously good at martial arts though, and was bound to be in the team.

'But no one can keep on winning forever,' Matt said, shaking his head clear of these thoughts. 'I reckon we've got a chance.'

'They'll know they've been in a fight, that's for sure!' said Catarina.

'Just think – this time tomorrow, we'll be there,' said Olivier.

'Guess we'd better go and get packed,' said Shawn. 'Early start in the morning.'

'Boy, are you lucky!' said Johnny.

Matt turned. He'd been standing by the landscape window of his room, gazing out at Beijing; he hadn't heard his room-mate come in. The sky was dark and the skyscrapers were ablaze with light. It was a spectacular sight, but this time tomorrow he'd be looking at a very different view – the city

where he'd grown up. He had already
phoned his mum to tell her the good news
and she'd been thrilled for him. He couldn't
wait to see London again – the River
Thames, the giant pencil-shape of Canary
Wharf and the glittering cylinder of the
Gherkin. He was looking forward to showing
the city to his friends.

'You've heard the news then?' said Matt.

'Yeah and am I jealous – I'd love to see
London!' Johnny said, throwing himself on to
his bed.

'Maybe you'll go there with the basketball
team one day,' said Matt.

'I sure hope so. You through with the
bathroom?'

'Yeah.'

'Goodnight then.'

Johnny got up and disappeared into the en
suite bathroom.

Matt yawned and pressed a button on the wall. The blinds smoothly descended, shutting out the glittering skyscrapers of Beijing.

He climbed into bed. Soothing, swirling patterns were projected on to the blind – a kaleidoscope of soft glowing colours. Matt watched them sleepily. As always, they had a hypnotic effect. He felt his eyes beginning to close. *This time tomorrow we'll be on the plane*, he thought. *This time tomorrow . . .*

Chapter 3

HEART OF A DIAMOND

'I can't believe we're here! In London!' said
Catarina excitedly.

'And this is just the airport,' said Matt. 'It
gets even better!'

His friends laughed.

'Come along, this way,' said Mr Figgis. He
was their history teacher and form tutor who
had accompanied the team, along with
Chang. 'Stick together.'

The team followed the two teachers
through passport control and out into the

arrivals lounge. A crowd stood behind the barrier, waiting to greet the newly arrived passengers. Many held placards with the name of the person they were waiting for. Matt's jaw dropped in surprise as he saw one of the placards said MATT JAMES. And holding it was his –

'Mum!' said Matt.

Smiling, his mum pushed through the crowd towards him. 'Surprised?' She threw her arms around him and hugged him.

'Great to see you, Mum! But –' He gently disentangled himself. It *was* great to see her, but a bit embarrassing too. The whole team was watching.

'Isn't that sweet!' said Carl mockingly. 'The little boy's reunited with his mummy and – oof!'

Catarina had just given him a violent shove in the back.

'Now now, settle down, no pushing!' said Mr Figgis.

'But, Mum, what are you doing here? I thought –'

'I was still in Beijing? The embassy sent me to London for a meeting, so I decided to surprise you!'

Matt grinned. He had a feeling his mother might have deliberately arranged the embassy meeting, once she knew he was coming to London. 'That's just great!'

'Isn't it? And I thought we could stay with Grandma and Grandad – they'd love to see you again.'

'I'm afraid that will not be possible, Mrs James,' said Chang politely. 'It is most necessary that Matt stays with squad. There will be time for visits after the tournament. But as captain, Matt must be with the squad.'

'Captain? Oh well, of course – in that

35

case . . .' She turned to Matt. 'You didn't tell me you were captain!'

'Only for this one tournament,' muttered Carl sourly.

'Could you squeeze in one little visit before the contest?' Mrs James asked. 'There's a party at the embassy tomorrow night and I'd like to invite the whole squad. Teachers included, of course. Would that be possible?'

Matt looked at Chang Sifu, hoping he'd say yes.

Chang gave a small bow. Mr Figgis nodded enthusiastically.

'We accept,' said Chang. 'It will be an honour to attend. But we shall not be able to stay late. Team need their rest. And now, we should make our way to hotel.'

He looked pointedly at Matt. Matt suddenly realized that as captain, it was his responsibility to lead the team out of here.

'OK, team,' he said. 'This way.'

He said goodbye to his mother and strode through the concourse to the exit. Outside, a gleaming silver double-decker coach was waiting for them. Passers-by cast admiring, curious glances at the squad of eleven young athletes in their red Beijing Academy tracksuits. Matt felt a surge of pride to be captaining them. He saw the team on to the coach and was the last to board.

Chang Sifu and Mr Figgis sat at the front downstairs. Matt joined the team upstairs. He sat next to Shawn, with Catarina and Olivier in the seat behind.

'London, here we come!' said Catarina, as the coach pulled away. The squad whooped and cheered in excitement.

'You'll have to show us the sights, Matt,' said Shawn.

'Sure,' said Matt. 'If you look out of the

window on your left, there's Buckingham Palace!'

'No kidding!' said Shawn, staring out of the window at the large white building they were passing. 'Really?'

'No!' grinned Matt. 'It's only the Hoover Building!'

Everyone roared with laughter. Except Carl, who tutted loudly and took out a karate magazine.

As the son of an ambassador, Matt was used to official parties and receptions. But this one seemed particularly impressive. The embassy building was in a square in Kensington – a white mansion, four storeys high, with great tall double doors, and a uniformed doorman in a top hat. He bowed as the Beijing team passed.

'Whoa,' said Catarina. 'Will you look at this place?'

'This is quite something, Matt,' said Shawn.

'Isn't it?' said Matt. He realized his palms were sweating.

A curved marble staircase led up to the reception. Along the walls hung portraits in gilt frames, of lords and ladies and generals. Matt noticed Chang looking around with interest as they ascended the stairs. *It must look as exotic to him as the Forbidden City does to me*, thought Matt.

They passed through into a great hall with a polished parquet floor, twinkling chandeliers and high windows that overlooked the green square. The room was full of people in smart suits and evening dresses. There was a loud buzz of conversation and laughter, and a string quartet was playing classical music.

Across the room, Matt saw his mother. She had her hair pinned up and she was wearing a

39

shimmering blue evening dress and a glittering diamond necklace. Matt watched her chatting, gracefully moving from one group to the next. Matt caught her eye and she gave him a small wave, but he didn't go up and speak to her yet; she might look like she was having fun, but he knew that to an ambassador, meeting and greeting people was all part of the job.

Waitresses in black dresses with little white aprons were circulating with trays of canapés – prawns on skewers, tiny triangles of toast with caviar, miniature chocolate puddings – and glasses of champagne and soft drinks.

'This is the life!' said Olivier.

Most of the Beijing team stood together in a cluster, sipping orange juice. Carl and Andrei stood a little way off.

'Do you think everyone's having a good time?' Matt asked the other Tigers.

'They ought to, with food like this,' said

Olivier, as he took a canapé from a passing waitress.

'What's this one?' asked Catarina, her hand hovering over a canapé with a sliver of something bright red on top.

'I'd be careful of that one – it's got raw chilli on, by the look of it!' said Olivier.

'How come you know so much about these things?' asked Shawn.

'I've been to tons of these things with my dad,' said Olivier.

Matt caught sight of a familiar figure on the other side of the room – a boy about his own age, stocky, with curly hair and a broad friendly face. 'Hey, Harry!'

He made his way through the throng of guests. Harry's face lit up.

'Matt! What are you doing here?'

'I'm in London for the tournament. With your lot! You in the team?'

'I certainly am! So we're gonna be up against each other? This is going to be interesting!'

'Come and meet the rest of the Beijing team – you'll like them, they're a great bunch of guys.'

Matt led Harry over to the squad. 'This is my old friend Harry Vincent-Bennett. We were at school together before BIA.'

'Good to meet you, Harry,' said Olivier, politely shaking hands.

'Hi, Harry,' said Catarina.

'He's going to be fighting against us in the tournament,' Matt explained.

'Yeah?' said Shawn. 'What's your martial art?'

'Tae kwon-do. Took it up at the same time as Matt – and I taught him everything he knows!' grinned Harry.

'You wish!' said Matt.

The rest of the Beijing squad – Wolfgang, Lola, Jahmal and the others – gathered round to greet Matt's friend. The only one who did not join in was Carl, who folded his arms and turned away. 'I don't want to talk to the opposition, thanks very much!' he said in a loud voice.

'Carl,' said Matt, 'that's stupid. Harry's my friend, and there's no need –'

'You're supposed to be the captain!' Carl fired back. 'You should set an example, not be hobnobbing with the enemy!'

'Harry!' said a voice even louder than Carl's. 'What do you think you're playing at?'

A twinge of dread ran through Matt. *I know that voice*, he thought. He turned to see Adam Bates. His chin was held high and his eyes had the same stony stare Matt remembered. He hadn't changed at all since Matt had seen him last – except that he was taller now. He was easily as tall as Catarina (who was the tallest of the Beijing squad) and much more heavily built, with broad shoulders and thick arms and legs.

Most members of the Beijing team took a step away from Adam. They could sense he was trouble. But only Matt knew just how much trouble Adam could be.

'What do you think you're doing, Harry?' repeated Adam. He grabbed Harry by the arm. 'We don't talk to these guys.'

'Wait a minute,' said Catarina. 'Who are you?'

'I'm the captain of the Kensington International Academy martial arts team. The team that's gonna give you the hammering of a lifetime!'

Matt knew, as captain, he had to respond to this challenge. He placed himself squarely before Adam. 'You think so, do you?'

Recognition dawned in Adam's eyes. Then he laughed. 'Little Matt James! Wow, your team must really be scraping the barrel if you got in! I tell you what, the stuff you went through in school is gonna be nothing, *nothing*, compared to what's gonna happen to you in the tournament. Remember what I used to do to you in the playground? Imagine that but double it.'

'A lot's changed since then,' said Matt quietly.

'I don't think so. Come on, Harry. Don't waste any more time talking to these no-hopers.' Adam dragged Harry by the collar and pulled him away. Before he turned to go, he paused and eyeballed Matt stonily, without speaking.

Matt met his gaze.

Then Adam turned on his heel and pushed through the crowd, knocking into one of the waitresses.

'He's not gonna get away with that!' said Catarina and started after Adam.

Matt caught her by the arm. 'Leave it,' he said. 'We don't want to start anything here. It's better to save it up. Beating him in the tournament will hurt him more than anything.'

Lola said in a clear voice, 'I don't like that boy.'

Her remark broke the tension and everyone laughed.

'I don't like him much either,' said Matt.

'The guy's a complete jerk!' said Carl. 'But why was he going on about the stuff you went through in school?'

'He was the worst bully in our primary school,' said Matt. 'He used to give lots of kids a hard time, me included.'

'And he's bragging about it?' said Shawn incredulously. 'You'd think he'd be embarrassed.'

Matt shrugged. 'He's always been that way. Thinks he's the best. His dad's Frank Bates, the diamond merchant – he's super-rich, and Adam's always been spoilt.'

'Yeah, but I can't believe you let him bully you!' said Carl.

'I didn't *let* him –'

'You shoulda just hit the guy!'

'It was before I took up tae kwon-do.'

'So what? You gotta stand up for yourself. People who get bullied deserve everything they get, that's what I reckon!'

'That's the dumbest thing I ever heard,' said Catarina.

'Off-the-scale dumb,' agreed Olivier.

The rest of the team nodded or murmured agreement.

Carl went red. He reached and grabbed a canapé from a passing waitress and stuffed it into his mouth. A moment later his face went crimson – he'd grabbed the one with raw chilli.

Matt watched Carl rush off to get some water, and shook his head pityingly, 'What is he like?'

'Changing the subject,' said Catarina, 'look at Master Chang. Looks kinda left out, no?'

Matt saw that Chang Sifu was standing in a corner on his own with a slightly lost air, clutching a glass. *He probably isn't used to parties like this*, thought Matt.

'Let's go and talk to him,' said Matt to the other Tigers.

Chang greeted them with a faint smile.

'Are you enjoying yourself, Sifu?' asked Shawn.

'It is . . . interesting,' replied Chang. 'Well done, Matt, for not reacting when Kensington captain tried to provoke. A horse may jump if stung by a wasp; but still, it remains a horse, while the wasp is only a wasp.'

'But how did you —?' said Matt, then stopped. There was no point asking how Chang knew what had happened between him and Adam. He knew by now that Chang noticed absolutely everything.

'He was horrible,' said Catarina. 'I dunno how someone like that can bear to exist!'

'Sometimes,' said Chang gravely, 'the heart of a diamond does not shine as bright as its face.'

'Doesn't it?' said Matt. He was about to ask what Chang meant by this when he felt a tap on the shoulder. He turned to see his mother standing there, the light shining off her diamond necklace.

'Matt, your uncle Martin and aunt Rosamund from the States are here. They haven't seen you since you were five — they want to meet you!'

'OK,' said Matt, following his mother.

'Well, well,' said Uncle Martin. 'Here's Matt! Who's been stretching you then?'

'Sorry?'

'When you were five you were only this big,' said Aunt Rosamund, holding her hand at waist-height. 'But now you're as tall as me!'

'Yes, I – I suppose I've grown,' said Matt.

'You certainly have!'

The grown-ups asked him a few more questions about Beijing, then started to talk about his mother's necklace.

'It's magnificent!' said Aunt Rosamund.

'Fine piece of work,' said Uncle Martin knowledgeably. 'Excellent quality, anyone can see that. How did you, er –'

'It's not mine, I'm afraid,' said Matt's mother. 'I only wish it were. I've hired it for the evening – from the Bates Diamond

Company. This is so spectacular I just wanted
to be able to wear it tonight.' Matt's mother
stroked the jewels at her throat.

Matt looked at the necklace. The Bates
Diamond Company was Adam's father's firm.
The necklace certainly was spectacular. *You
almost need shades to look at it*, thought Matt.
There were three layers of diamonds,
threaded on fine gold chains. The diamonds
were very large and caught the light in the
most amazing way – almost as if the light
shone out from inside them, rather than
being reflected off their surface.

'Weird to think those diamonds are
basically just little pieces of coal, isn't it?' said
a voice close by. It was Shawn, who'd
squeezed his way through the throng.

'Coal?' Matt asked.

'Yeah, diamonds are just carbon – the same
stuff coal's made of,' said Shawn. 'But when

it's really, really compressed by geological forces, you get diamond. The hardest substance known to man. You know the only thing that can scratch a diamond?'

Matt thought briefly. 'Er – another diamond?'

'Right! And –'

CRASH!

A huge splintering *thud* cut right through the murmur of conversation. Matt spun round and saw that one of the high windows was smashed; shards of glass still bounced and skittered on the parquet floor.

A black-clad figure came swinging into the room.

There were screams and shouts, as all the guests started back from the intruder.

'Look out!'

'Who is it?'

'Call the police!'

The intruder was dressed from head to toe in black, face covered completely with only a slit for the eyes. A ninja warrior – Matt recognized the outfit. What was going on? Some sort of stunt? A Ninjagram?

The man ran across the room and took a flying leap. He landed on top of a wall cabinet some two metres tall. He reached for a fuse box high on the wall, flung it open and ripped out the fuses.

The room was plunged into darkness.

More screams.

Matt realized this wasn't a stunt.

The intruder jumped down and did a series of acrobatic handsprings and cartwheels across the room. In the semi-darkness he gave the eerie impression of a large, fast-moving animal with too many legs.

The guests scrambled to get out of his way. Adam Bates dived under a table.

Instinctively, Matt moved closer to his mother to protect her. She was standing with her hands pressed to her cheeks, frozen in shock.

The intruder was approaching them. In one smooth motion, he landed from his final cartwheel and shoved Matt out of the way. Matt's mother turned, trying to escape.

'Get away!' she cried. With the speed of a striking snake, the man's hand shot out. There was a clinking sound and a gasp of terror.

Then the intruder was tumbling and cartwheeling his way towards the window. He dived through, and was gone.

But we're on the second floor, thought Matt. *How did he —?*

His mother let out a cry. Her hand flew to her throat.

'The necklace! It's gone!'

Someone had brought a lamp into the room. Matt saw a red mark on his mother's throat where the necklace had been ripped away.

There were gasps of consternation.

'What am I going to do?' said Matt's mother, her voice cracking.

More lights were being brought into the room. Adam crawled out from under the table. A babble of talk burst out. Matt heard the word 'Scorpion!' muttered by several people and wondered what they meant. A tall grey-haired man was saying, 'Calm down! Everyone calm down!' Matt recognized him as Sir Hubert Tremayne, Head of the Ambassadorial Service.

'Mum – are you all right?' Matt went to his mother and put his arm round her. 'He didn't hurt you?'

'No, no, but the necklace is priceless, it's worth millions! What will the Bates Diamond

Company say – they're going to be furious!'

A hot anger rose within Matt. He wasn't going to let this happen to his mum. The thief wouldn't get away with it! Matt wasn't bothered about the necklace, but he was bothered that his mother was so upset.

'This is an outrage!' boomed the voice of Sir Hubert Tremayne. 'Appalling! Has anybody called the police?'

But by the time the police got here, Matt realized, the thief would be long gone.

'Come on!' he said to Shawn.

They ran to the window. Catarina and Olivier arrived there at the same time. They peered out through the shattered window. Just outside was a tall plane tree.

'That must have been his escape route,' said Matt.

The square was lit by yellow street-lamps. It appeared to be empty.

'He can't have got very far,' said Catarina. 'Let's go!'

She thrust her leg over the window sill and leapt into the air. She caught hold of a branch of the tree and swung herself down. Shawn and Olivier quickly followed.

Matt's turn.

Before he went through, he cast a glance back into the room. His mother was being looked after by Sir Hubert and friends. There was still such confusion that no one would possibly notice four kids climbing out of a window.

No one except Chang Sifu.

He was standing in the corner, looking in Matt's direction. It was difficult to see, with only the light from the street-lamps outside to go by, but Matt was pretty sure that Chang gave him a nod of approval.

Here goes! thought Matt. With all the climbing he'd done in his adventures with the Tangshan Tigers, he'd lost his old fear of heights. He launched himself out of the window, two storeys above the pavement below.

It was time to catch a thief.

THE CHASE

Matt caught at a branch, swung giddily in the air for a moment, and found a foothold. He steadied himself. From here he had a good view of the whole square. He glimpsed a dark figure running down one of the streets that led off from it.

He climbed down the tree rapidly but carefully, making sure that he always had at least three points of contact with the branches while the fourth limb searched for a handhold or foothold. He jumped from the lowest branch to join his friends in the square below, who were waiting expectantly.

'Did you see which way he went?' asked Olivier.

'That way!' said Matt.

They set off at a sprint. Catarina and Olivier, the two fastest runners, led the way. Just as they left the square Matt heard his mother's voice calling after him: 'Matt! Come back!'

He glanced back to see his mother leaning dangerously far out of the window.

Matt couldn't tell whether she'd seen him, but he didn't even think about stopping. His blood was up – he wanted to nail the thief who'd attacked his mother.

He pelted down the street after the others, footsteps echoing on the pavement, past terraces of elegant Georgian houses.

At the end they had a choice. A road that

led to a brightly lit main street, or a narrow cobbled alley.

'He'd look pretty conspicuous out on the main road in that ninja gear!' said Matt.

'Gotta be the alley then!' said Shawn.

They clattered over the cobblestones. A cat yowled and leapt on to a roof as they passed.

The alley led into a maze of side streets.

'Better split and try them all,' said Matt. 'Shout out if you see him!'

'Check!' said Shawn.

They ran off in different directions. Matt went down a back street lined with wheelie bins. He leapt over recycling boxes as he ran. The street curved round to the left and Matt found himself running past the back doors to a line of restaurants; a man in a chef's hat looked up in surprise as Matt ran by.

He reached the end and stopped to look left and right. Olivier was coming towards him.

'No sign?'

'Nothing,' said Matt.

'Let's try this way!'

Together they ran up the street. Olivier was a fast runner, but Matt, breathing hard, was able to keep up. A good job he'd done so much martial arts training – it had kept him super-fit.

Again, Matt saw the bright lights of the main road ahead. He and Olivier slowed to a halt. They heard running footsteps and saw Shawn coming round the corner.

'No luck?'

'Nowhere to be seen. The guy's totally disappeared!'

'He must know these streets like the back of his hand,' said Matt.

Catarina's voice rang out in the distance. 'Guys? Where are you?'

'Coming!'

They doubled back and ran in the
direction of her voice. She was just emerging
from another alley. 'He didn't come this way,'
she gasped. 'No way out.'

'We've tried everywhere else,' said Matt.
'We'd better go back.'

'But he must be somewhere!' said Catarina.

'Yeah, but not round here any more,' said
Olivier. 'We've lost him.'

'No one escapes from the Tangshan Tigers!'
said Catarina.

'We'll get him,' promised Matt, though he
couldn't help feeling disappointed. 'We'll
track him down. Somehow.'

They made their way back to the square
where the embassy building was. Catarina
immediately started to climb the tree.

'Wait,' said Matt. 'We'd better use the door
this time.'

He had a hunch his mother might be cross

with him. And swinging back in through the broken window would probably not help.

'Are you out of your mind?' Matt's mother demanded. 'Climbing out of a second-storey window, chasing after a thief. You could have been badly hurt – or worse!'

All around, guests were getting ready to leave. The string quartet had stopped playing and a cleaner was sweeping up the broken glass. Two uniformed police were taking witness statements and contact details of the guests.

'It's OK, we can look after ourselves, Mum –'

'Don't be ridiculous! How could you look after yourself if you'd fallen from the tree? Or if you'd caught up with that man and he'd pulled a knife on you? This isn't a game, Matt!'

Matt wished that he could tell his mother about the Tangshan Tigers, and how they'd come through far more dangerous situations and faced far more dangerous enemies in the past – but that would only make matters worse. He hung his head and mumbled, 'Sorry, Mum.'

Out of the corner of his eye Matt noticed Chang Sifu watching. Chang gave a tiny nod of sympathy, and made his way over to Matt and his mother.

'We should start to move back to hotel,' he said. 'We have busy day tomorrow. Thank you very much for excellent party, Mrs James – a pity it finished in such an unpleasant way.'

'Yes, it wasn't quite what I'd expected,' said Mrs James. 'Well, goodnight. And good luck in the tournament,' she added. She moved forward and hugged her son. 'I'm sorry I snapped, Matt. It's only because I'm worried about you; you know that, don't you?'

Matt felt her tears against his cheek. 'I know, Mum,' he said 'It's OK; don't worry.'

Half the guests had already gone and the other half were in the process of leaving. As the Beijing squad followed Chang and Mr Figgis downstairs, Matt saw people pulling on their coats, nervously peering out of the front door to check the coast was clear.

While he and the Tigers were waiting to pick up their coats at the cloakroom, Adam Bates came past. He eyed Matt contemptuously before speaking.

'Your mum's gonna be in big trouble, James. My dad doesn't like people losing his diamonds.'

'She didn't lose the necklace – it was stolen! Anyway, it was insured, wasn't it?'

'Yeah, but my dad charges a penalty when

clients are negligent. I reckon your poor old mum's gonna have to pay a big fat fine!'

'She wasn't negligent –'

'Get out of here! She wore the necklace in a public place, knowing the Scorpion was around –'

'Who's the Scorpion?' asked Shawn.

'You guys don't know much, do you? The Scorpion's the most famous jewel thief in London. The police are baffled – no one can stop him – he's in the papers all the time. Haven't you seen this?' Adam took out a brand-new iPhone and clicked on to a news screen. SCORPION STRIKES AGAIN, the headline said. 'See?'

'Hey, let's have a look,' said Shawn.

He reached out for the phone, but Adam pulled it away and put it in his pocket. 'Don't touch what you can't afford!' He turned back to Matt. 'So with the Scorpion around, your mum decides to wear a priceless diamond necklace out to a party in London – that wasn't too clever, was it?'

For a moment Matt was too angry to speak. He felt a muscle in his jaw twitching. But he was determined not to rise to the bait. He'd been bullied once by Adam – he wasn't going to let Adam get the advantage over him ever again.

'See you at the tournament, Adam,' Matt said pleasantly, as he picked up his coat.

'Hey, come back here,' said Adam. 'I haven't finished!'

'Oh yes, you have,' said Matt as he kept walking.

'You handled that well,' Olivier said to him as they climbed the steps of the team coach.

'Thanks.'

'Will your mom really have to pay a fine?' asked Shawn.

'That's not going to happen!' said Matt. 'And do you know why?'

'Yeah,' said Catarina. 'Because we're gonna catch the Scorpion, right?'

'Right,' said Matt. 'There's no way he attacks my mum and gets away with it. And there's no way he's going to get the better of the Tangshan Tigers!'

As the coach pulled away, Matt gazed out of the back window at the London streets and squares and alleys. Somewhere out there, perhaps not too far away, was the Scorpion. And sooner or later, the Tangshan Tigers would find him . . .

It was breakfast time in the hotel early the following morning. Matt had been tempted by the aroma of bacon and eggs, but resisted.

Instead he had a roll and butter, orange juice, and a banana and kiwi fruit. Plenty of carbohydrates and vitamins – that was what Chang always recommended in the run-up to a tournament. Except that he didn't call them that; he called them fruits of the earth and fruits of the trees.

Most of the team had followed Matt's example – except for Carl, who'd ordered a full English breakfast.

'I wonder what Chang's got lined up for us today?' said Olivier.

'I hope we can see some of the sights of London!' said Lola, as she poured herself a glass of apple juice.

'But don't we need to train?' said Wolfgang, buttering some toast.

'And don't *we* need to get on with finding the Scorpion?' whispered Shawn to the rest of the Tangshan Tigers.

'All wishes will be satisfied,' said Chang, who had silently materialized by their table. Matt wondered if their teacher had heard what Matt had said the night before, but if he had he gave no sign.

'Kensington International Academy will provide us with our toughest match yet. Training is essential. But we have no training facilities in this hotel, and Kensington facilities not made available to us until tomorrow. Therefore, today, London itself will be our training ground.'

'How do you mean, Sifu?' asked Matt.

'You will find out,' said Chang. 'Report to team bus in hotel car park in half an hour.'

As the team finished their breakfast, Matt and the rest of the Tangshan Tigers gathered in a huddle by the door.

'Training first. Then we find out who this Scorpion is. Agreed?' said Matt.

He held out his fist. Shawn, Olivier and Catarina all brought their own fists down on top of his.

'Agreed!'

The team jumped off the bus at Tower Hill. It was a warm sunny day. The sunshine illuminated the pale grey stone of the Tower of London, and the passing cars and bikes sparkled in the light. A little further off, Tower Bridge rose into the blue sky above the River Thames.

'Hey, that's one cool castle!' said Catarina, pointing at the Tower of London. 'How old is it?'

'Oh, about nine hundred years,' said Matt. It was strange that he should feel proud of the Tower – after all, he had had nothing to do with building it – but it was part of his home town.

'Gather round,' said Chang Sifu. The team congregated on a patch of emerald green lawn. 'Today we concentrate on extending *Chi Sao* training.'

'You mean sparring?' said Carl, brightening up. 'Like we did last time, with our arms touching?'

'Not sparring today. Instead, we have exercise to improve physical sensitivity. All you need to do is walk side by side with partner, arms touching at all times –'

'But what's the point of that?' demanded Carl. 'We might as well stroll around eating ice creams – improve our physical sensitivity to chocolate and vanilla –'

'Training is to improve awareness of another body and its movements – and hence awareness of possible opponent. You are unlikely to be fighting ice cream in tournament.'

There was a burst of laughter from the squad. Matt enjoyed the calm easy way Chang put Carl in his place.

Chang finished explaining the task as he led the team towards Tower Bridge, past hordes of tourists armed with camcorders. 'You will walk length of bridge, up and down, in pairs. Arms touching. You will be joined by imaginary elastic cord at waist. Let us see, you are eleven, so we need one group of three. Lola, Wolfgang and Olivier, yes.'

With deft fingers he mimed attaching an invisible cord that linked Lola's waist to Wolfgang's, and Wolfgang's to Olivier's. 'You see, cord is short, if stretched it will break. So you must maintain contact at all times, or cord will break! But you will be walking through crowds, you will have to make sudden changes of pace or direction. Are there any questions?'

Jahmal put up his hand. 'Won't we look a bit silly, sir?'

'Too right we will,' muttered Carl.

'That is of no importance,' said Chang smoothly. 'Martial artist must put ego to one side. If you feel embarrassed, then embarrassment must be conquered. Now, please form into these pairs.' As Chang spoke, he attached an imaginary cord joining each pair: 'Matt and Andrei, Paolo and Abdul, Jahmal and Shawn, and Carl and Catarina.'

'Oh great,' said Carl sarcastically.

'Yes, it is great,' said Catarina. 'For you, not for me!'

Matt remembered how distrustful he used to feel about Andrei, who was an unpredictable character. He had once attempted to knock out a whole auditorium full of people with sleeping gas. But under Chang's influence, Andrei seemed to have settled down.

They stood side by side on the walkway of the bridge, as taxis and buses rumbled past on the road beside them. Both rolled up their sleeves. They touched arms. Behind and in front of them, the other pairs were doing the same thing, drawing curious glances from passers-by. A party of Japanese schoolgirls giggled, their hands covering their mouths. Andrei nodded at Matt, and they began walking.

It took a special kind of concentration, Matt found. He felt Andrei's arm against his as they moved along. He could keep pace with Andrei's movements as long as he didn't think about them. He had to trust his body to respond, not his mind.

Andrei accelerated to get past a slow-walking dad holding hands with a pair of toddlers. Simultaneously, Matt quickened his step to keep pace.

Matt had to move abruptly to the right to avoid a party of loud-voiced Italian teenagers who were coming towards them, taking up most of the pavement. Andrei veered with him, his arm never leaving Matt's, as if they were both following the same track.

A boy cycled towards them, merrily ringing his bell. He went straight for the middle of them and for a second it looked as if they'd have to pull apart, but at the last moment both instinctively swerved in the same direction – to the left – and contact was unbroken.

It worked, Matt realized. He could *feel* Andrei's movements – he didn't need to second-guess them.

They passed Carl and Catarina. Carl wasn't talking now; he looked to be concentrating as he tried to second-guess Catarina's rapid, unpredictable movements. Not for the first time, Matt thought, Carl was finding that Chang's training exercises were not as easy as they seemed.

Then Matt's attention was caught by a sudden commotion on the River Thames below. A speedboat was roaring along at breakneck speed, its prow lifted clear of the water. It was a beautiful craft, blue and silver, gleaming in the sunshine, and it was weaving in and out of larger boats, often with centimetres to spare, making smaller craft pitch and toss as it passed. Matt could just make out the driver – a man dressed in black, wearing a baseball cap, hunched over the wheel.

Intrigued, Matt forgot what he was doing and moved over to the side of the bridge to see better. His movement was so abrupt that he broke contact with Andrei completely.

'Hey!' said Andrei.

'Oh, sorry! I was just –'

As Matt watched, the speedboat disappeared under the bridge, then reappeared on the other side, churning up a creamy wake behind it as it raced towards Greenwich.

'Important not to let mind wander, Matt,' said Chang's quiet voice. He had appeared on the walkway beside them. 'If you try to do too many things at once, you will do nothing well.'

Matt turned back from the bridge. It looked like he was still letting distractions get to him after all.

'Perhaps you'll do better next time,' scoffed Carl. 'If you work, like, a *million* years.' Matt glanced at the other Tangshan Tigers. Catarina rolled her eyes and Olivier shrugged. Shawn came up beside Carl.

'Yes, he might even become as average as

you, Carl,' he said, grinning. Then he broke into a run across the bridge with Carl chasing after him.

Later, they walked back past the Tower of London to where the team bus was waiting for them. It was time to go to the Kensington International Academy. Matt fell into step with Chang Sifu. He had enjoyed the training and felt that he was getting better at the *Chi Sao* technique.

'How will *Chi Sao* help in a combat situation, Sifu?'

'*Chi Sao* will aid you in anticipating opponents' movements,' said Chang. 'Feeling their intentions before they act.'

'But when we're actually in the tournament, our opponent isn't going to co-operate; they're not going to be maintaining contact at all times –'

'Not knowingly – but it is certain that Kensington team will try to fight at close quarters. They will force physical contact upon you. I know this because I know their coach – Kawada-san. A well-respected, highly honourable Japanese master of ju-jitsu. Close-quarters fighting is his style. I know: I have faced him in international competition twice.'

They were walking past the gate to the Tower. Big black ravens strutted about on the lawn. Two Yeomen Warders in red uniforms stood on either side of the gate. Matt noticed that one of them caught Chang's eye and gave a respectful nod, which Chang returned. Perhaps there was something in Chang's bearing that automatically drew admiration, thought Matt.

'Did you beat Kawada-san?' asked Matt.

'He was a tough opponent,' said Chang.

'On one occasion I beat him, yes. On the other occasion he beat me.'

Carl had come up to join them. 'But can't we just stand off, pick them off when they try to come in?' he asked. 'I'm a *karateka*, and Matt does tae kwon-do – we're trained to fight at long range.'

Chang Sifu inclined his head. 'Normally this would be wise tactic. But Kawada-san will be prepared. His team will be instructed to get in close. They are home team and will seek to dominate. I do not want to fight defensively – I want to match them at own game.'

'Right,' said Carl thoughtfully. 'OK.'

A moment later, after Chang had walked on ahead, Carl said: 'That's what I like to hear – fighting talk! That's something I can really get behind.'

'Me too,' said Matt. He wondered if it was

possibly the first time he'd ever agreed with Carl. And who knew? This new training might help Matt and the rest of the Tigers if they ever came up against the Scorpion. *Correction*, thought Matt. *When we come up against the Scorpion.*

STUNG!

'Wow!' said Shawn as the team bus pulled up on the gravel drive the next morning. 'It looks really old – like a stately home!'

The Kensington International Academy was very different from the Beijing International Academy. It was a massive redbrick building with steps ascending to a grand porch supported by Greek columns. It stood in its own wooded grounds.

'Yeah, it's quite a place, isn't it?' said Matt. Even having grown up surrounded by historic buildings, he found this place impressive.

The team piled off the bus and followed Master Chang up the broad marble steps. At the top they were greeted by two men: Mr Mulbarton, the Headmaster, and Kawada-san. Mr Mulbarton was a tall man with a slight stoop, grey hair and a red bow tie. Kawada-san was shorter but very compact and well built – he looked strong and resilient, as though he was made of toughened rubber. He was wearing a dark suit and had a small black beard.

Kawada-san bowed to Chang, who returned the bow. Matt noticed that they looked at each other with mutual respect – two old rivals meeting again after many years.

Mr Mulbarton shook hands with Chang and said: 'Welcome. And may the best team win.'

'I am sure it will be a fine contest,' said

85

Kawada-san. 'Any team coached by Master Chang will be a formidable force.'

'I am sure, likewise, any team coached by Kawada-san will be of the very highest quality,' said Chang with equal politeness.

'Our team is using the *dojo* for practice at this moment,' said Kawada-san. 'I will be coaching them there for the rest of the morning. But you are welcome to use the facilities after lunch. Until then, do treat the place as your own. All the facilities are at your disposal. There is a gym, a swimming pool – as well as a cafeteria, a recreation room, a library, and of course the rooms you've been allocated. Some of my students will be happy to show you around.'

Three boys showed up, wearing the smart green jackets of the Kensington Academy uniform. Their teacher nodded at them once, then walked away. Matt recognized one of the boys at once – Philip Stanton, a boy he'd known at primary school.

'Hey, Philip!'

'Great to see you, Matt!'

'These are my friends – Catarina, Shawn, Olivier, meet Phil.'

'Hi there. Well, where do you want to go?'

'The library,' said Matt immediately. He saw the other Tangshan Tigers nod in agreement – they knew what he had in mind.

Carl turned round in disbelief. 'The library? What do you want to go there for, you boffin? Why not the gym, or –'

'I like libraries,' said Matt. 'Good places for finding things out.'

'Same old Matt,' Philip laughed, clapping him on the back. 'You love your books. Used to love reading adventure stories, didn't you? Come on, I'll show you the way.'

Matt shared a secret glance with the other

Tangshan Tigers. Philip had no idea that Matt didn't just read adventure stories these days – he had the adventures himself!

Most of the squad either went to the gym or the recreation room – the other two Kensington boys showed them the way. Before Chang moved away he paused and looked at the Tangshan Tigers.

'Do not spend too long in library,' he said. 'Learning is good. But so too is action.'

Was he talking about the tournament – or did he have some idea of their plans to deal with the Scorpion? With Chang, there was no way of knowing.

Chang turned and headed towards the staffroom with Kawada-san, with Mr Figgis trailing along behind. As they left, Matt heard the two martial arts teachers reminiscing about a tournament they had both attended in Thailand.

Philip took the Tangshan Tigers up to the library, which was on the second floor, up a broad curving staircase with gold-painted banisters.

'What's the plan, then, guys?' whispered Catarina. 'Gonna do something clever on a computer, Shawn?'

'No need to be too clever – should be pretty straightforward,' said Shawn.

Matt chatted with Philip about the tournament. Philip didn't do martial arts, but was naturally rooting for his school. Except in the case of Adam Bates.

'I wish his opponent could take him down a peg or two. But it's not likely to happen. He really is good. He's never lost a fight. But the whole school would thank you if you could beat him.'

'He's not too popular then?' said Matt.

'Nobody likes him,' said Philip. 'Well,

maybe his mum does, but that would be about it.'

'Why am I not surprised?' murmured Olivier.

They reached the library. It was an ultra-modern building with walls of tinted glass and an open space in the centre. You could look up and see galleries of bookshelves ascending above you. It was nearly empty – most of the Kensington pupils were in lessons, Matt guessed. But there were a few older students reading on the higher levels, and a librarian behind a desk who looked up when they came in. She had a long face and looked at them over her glasses as if daring them to make a noise.

'What did you want to do?' asked Philip quietly.

'We need a computer,' said Matt.

'Here, you can use any one,' said Philip.

There were banks of computers on desks all around. 'You'll need a username and password – you can use mine.'

'No need,' said Shawn briefly. He had already sat down at a terminal and his fingers were flying over the keyboard. 'These are easy to get into – just change the settings for the domain, then any username will do and you can create a new password.'

The screen lit up and the desktop appeared. 'See?' grinned Shawn.

'Wow!' said Philip. 'You look like you know what you're doing! I'll leave you to it then.'

'Thanks,' said Matt. 'Catch you later, Phil.'

When Phil had gone, Catarina said: 'OK, so we gonna find out everything we can about this Scorpion dude, yes? You gonna do an Internet search, Shawn?'

'If I just key in "Scorpion" we'll get

hundreds of hits and most of it will be irrelevant,' said Shawn. 'I have some software for a more refined search, if I just download it.' As he spoke, he was moving the mouse around and clicking busily. Soon the words DOWNLOAD COMPLETE appeared on the screen. 'Now, if I enter "Scorpion", "diamonds", "theft" – and some parameters for dates, say the last six months – we'll get a much better picture. Only relevant stuff, and nothing duplicated.'

He hit the Enter key. Matt saw the screen fill with details of news reports of the Scorpion's activities. Matt, Olivier and Catarina leaned over the monitor. Shawn clicked on the first report that came up. Then another, and another . . . The Scorpion had certainly been busy: there had been diamond thefts at the rate of two or three a month; and in all of them he'd got clean away.

'Hadn't someone better write all this down?' asked Olivier. 'There's a lot of information here.'

'That's OK,' said Matt. He tapped his forehead. 'I've got it all here.'

'Oh yes,' said Olivier. 'Your photographic memory – I forgot!'

The librarian looked up. 'Ssshh!'

'Sorry,' said Olivier, giving her his most charming smile.

'You have to keep quiet in here, you know. What's all the noise about?'

'We were just trying to find something on the computer,' said Olivier politely. 'They're so complicated, aren't they?'

'Let me help you,' said the librarian with a sigh. She got up from her desk.

'Quick,' said Matt in a low voice. 'Olivier, stall her – Shawn, log out!'

Shawn had downloaded a search

programme on to a school computer, which was probably against the rules. Plus, their crime-fighting activities were supposed to be a secret. If the librarian found out they were researching diamond thefts on the Internet, Matt was prepared to bet there'd be trouble.

Olivier intercepted the librarian and stood between her and the monitor. 'We went to the Tower of London today – such a fascinating place – and we wanted to find out more about it. You wouldn't know how old it is, would you?'

'It was built by William the Conqueror,' said the librarian. She seemed pleased to be able to show off her knowledge. 'The oldest parts are over nine hundred years old.'

'Really?' marvelled Olivier. 'That old?'

Shawn had logged out by now. Matt breathed a sigh of relief. The librarian moved past Olivier.

'But you haven't logged in!' she said.

'We couldn't work out how,' said Shawn.
'I don't really understand computers.'

Catarina stifled a giggle.

'It's perfectly simple,' said the librarian.
'Here, let me show you . . .'

She gave them a short tutorial on how to
search the Internet. Then she returned to her
desk. Shawn swivelled in his chair to face the
others. 'So,' he said quietly. 'What have we
got?'

'We're looking at fifteen separate thefts
here,' said Matt, 'but they all have plenty in
common. First, they always take place in
public. He doesn't sneak into people's houses
when they're not there – he strikes at parties,
receptions, film premieres and so on. Targets
the victim, snatches the loot, and away.
Another thing – did anyone else notice this?
– every time, it's people wearing diamonds

from the Bates Diamond Company that get targeted.'

'I noticed that!' said Catarina. 'You reckon he's got some sort of grudge against Bates?'

'It's possible,' said Matt thoughtfully. 'I don't enjoy talking to Adam, but maybe I should speak to him and find out if his dad has any enemies.'

'If he's anything like his son, he's bound to!' said Shawn.

Their voices had risen again. The librarian looked up.

'Sorry!' mouthed Olivier.

'Let's go somewhere we can talk,' said Matt in a low voice.

They found a reading space with comfy chairs and a low table with the day's newspapers near the door. One of the papers had a headline about the latest theft, Matt saw: STUNG AGAIN, above a picture of the embassy building with its broken window.

'Here's another funny thing,' said Matt. 'Each time, he seems to disappear into thin air.'

'I don't understand that,' said Olivier. 'I mean there are so many people in this city, and he's done it so often – you'd think at *some* point someone would spot where he goes.'

'People do spot him,' said Shawn. 'There are plenty of eyewitness descriptions – tall, fit, acrobatic guy dressed like a ninja – but no one can ever keep track of him. When they follow, he vanishes!'

'Like he did when we were chasing him,' said Matt. 'Here's something else – pretty obvious, but all the thefts have happened in London. I wonder whether, if we plotted where they all took place, and where he disappeared each time – marked them on a map, right? – we might start to see some sort of pattern.'

'That's a good idea,' said Shawn. 'It wouldn't take long. If I pulled up a street map of London and printed it off –'

At that moment, the library door opened and Chang Sifu stood there, wearing his white martial arts suit.

'*Dojo* is now at our disposal,' he said. 'It is time to start training.'

A CLUE?

'Enjoy your time in the library?' said Carl with a sneer. 'Learn a lot, did you?'

'Yes, thanks,' said Matt mildly. He wasn't in the mood for an argument with Carl.

The Beijing team had gathered outside the *dojo* and were waiting for the Kensington team to leave. The facilities were impressive, Matt saw – the *dojo* was spacious, modern, air-conditioned, and even larger than the *kwoon* at the Beijing Academy. There were two *tatami* mats instead of the usual one.

The door opened and the Kensington team came out, carrying their gear, hair wet from the shower. They all looked fit and strong and walked with a bold confidence. A team that was used to winning.

Harry broke away from his team-mates and came to greet Matt. 'Hey, how's it going? You'll love our *dojo* – it's a great place to train.'

'I've told you about this before!' came Adam's harsh voice. He strode over and pulled Harry's shoulder. 'We don't talk to the enemy, right? We let our fists and feet do the talking!'

Matt noticed that Adam was carrying a training pad of the most expensive kind – a body protector used in full-contact training. It was brand new and the best make on the market – the sort that normally only a professional martial artist would use.

'That's a pretty good body protector you've got there,' he said. 'Did your dad buy it?'

'No, it was my fairy godmother,' said Adam sarcastically. Matt counted to ten and waited to calm down. Chang Sifu had always taught him not to waste energy on useless emotions – like feeling irritated by bullies and show-offs.

'Well, I better get going,' said Adam. 'No time to talk to losers!'

Adam pulled back his sleeve with a flourish and looked at his watch. It was quite a watch – gold face, gold strap, multiple dials on the face. Matt heard Shawn catch his breath.

'Hey, I know that watch. That's the one that keeps time to a radio signal from Greenwich, isn't it? Accurate to within a second every million years?'

'That's right,' said Adam. 'What about it?'

'My dad designed that watch! There are

only ten of them in the world – and each
one has ten diamonds in it, right?'

'That's it. My dad picked it up for me –
he's made some important new contacts in
the diamond trade, and this was a little
something to sweeten a deal.' He smirked.
'Bet you wish you could afford one!'

He swaggered away and his team followed.
As he passed, Harry threw Matt an
apologetic glance.

Matt was thinking hard. So Bates had made
new contacts in the diamond trade? Could
the diamond thefts be the work of a
disappointed rival?

'Come,' said Chang, gesturing at the open
door. 'Let us begin.'

Matt was captain of the squad; he had to
lead his team. He put aside his
preoccupations and stepped into the *dojo*. It
was time for the final training session.

'To prepare for close-quarters tactics of Kensington squad,' said Chang, 'let us match specialists in take-down styles – judo, ju-jitsu – against stand-ups, such as karate, tae kwon-do, kung fu.'

Chang went round the *dojo*, lightly touching students on the shoulder to put them in pairs, and one group of three. Matt was partnered with Wolfgang, the stocky, red-headed German boy who was a judo specialist.

'Stand-up fighters – your opponent will try to come in and get to grips. Strike with long-range blows if you can, using centre line – this picks up points – but be prepared to fight at close quarters also. Use *Chi Sao* to feel and counter opponent's moves.' Chang clapped his hands. 'Go.'

Matt knew from the word go that today he wasn't in the zone. He tried to focus on the *Chi Sao* principles but he kept thinking about the Scorpion, and how the Tangshan Tigers could trace him. Side by side with this, his thoughts kept returning to Adam Bates – how he hoped to be matched against him in the tournament tomorrow and wipe the smirk off his face. But what if he fought him and didn't win? *What if Adam wins and laughs at me?* Matt wondered.

His footwork was clumsy, his reactions were slow. Wolfgang was not the sort of fighter you could afford to ease up against. He threw Matt once, then sent him crashing down on his back a second time.

Wolfgang helped him up. 'Come on, Matt – you're not trying today!'

Chang Sifu came across.

'Matt,' he said gently. 'You are captain and must set example. You are not focusing. Your mind is too busy. You must empty mind. Think through your body. You understand?'

Matt nodded.

'Breathe deeply. Calm yourself. All the things that trouble you, imagine them getting smaller and smaller . . . Then begin again.'

Matt took several deep breaths. He pictured the Scorpion and Adam becoming tiny, like insects, like microbes, like atoms. He focused on his body, muscles relaxed and ready for action.

'Ready?' said Wolfgang.

'Ready.'

This time, when Wolfgang came in to attack, Matt was fully focused. As they grappled together, Matt felt Wolfgang's movement against him and his body knew what to expect – and how to respond. When Wolfgang attempted a throw, Matt felt it coming, went with it, and shifted his balance at the last moment, so that it was Wolfgang who crashed to the mat.

'Better,' said Chang quietly. 'And Wolfgang, remember counter-move Matt used – you might need tomorrow.'

Wolfgang nodded. '*Ja*, I will remember.'

Thank goodness for training, Matt thought. In training there were always second chances. If you got something wrong, you could work at it until it came right.

In the tournament, though, he'd have to get it right first time.

After the session was over and they had showered and changed, the Tigers went back to the library. This time they chose a computer terminal well away from the helpful librarian. Shawn downloaded and printed a street map of London. He spread it on a desk under a lamp and they all gathered round. With the aid of Matt's photographic memory, Olivier marked in all the sites where the Scorpion had struck, and where he'd last been spotted before disappearing.

The result was a scattergun array of red dots all over London, from east to west, stretching across the centre to the suburbs.

'This isn't helping,' said Matt. 'I was hoping there'd be a centre to all this – maybe a hideout he always makes his way to – but these dots are too far apart for that!'

'Maybe he's got hideouts all over town?' suggested Catarina.

'Maybe . . .' said Matt doubtfully. 'But – nearly twenty hideouts? It doesn't seem likely. Olivier's right, it doesn't make sense the way he's always able to disappear no matter where he is – where does he disappear *to*?'

'There's no pattern to it,' complained Olivier.

'Wait!' said Shawn. He clicked his fingers excitedly. 'There *is* a pattern; look – all these dots are close to the River Thames. See? Just a few streets away, every time!'

Matt exhaled a long slow breath. 'Shawn, you've got it! Somehow he gets down to the river – that's how he escapes . . .' He remembered the speedboat he'd seen roaring down the Thames yesterday. 'He might be working with someone, an accomplice who's waiting in a speedboat. He jumps in and they're away!'

'Yes,' said Shawn. 'I bet that's it!'

'The problem is, how's this gonna help us catch him?' said Catarina. 'We can't patrol up and down the river all day – they're not gonna let us off the school grounds unsupervised, and even if they did –'

'No, that's right,' said Matt regretfully. They were not as close to catching the Scorpion as he'd thought. 'Unless we can find out where he's going to strike next . . .'

'And how we gonna do that?' asked Catarina.

'We're only in London another five days,' added Shawn. 'If we don't get a clue by then, that's it.'

'We'll have to think!' said Matt. 'And keep our eyes and ears open. At least we've made some progress.'

'That's true,' said Olivier. 'And, all this thinking has made me hungry – we've got the welcome dinner with Kensington tonight. Better go to our rooms and get changed.'

The dinner was held in a great hall with stained-glass windows, which gave it a cathedral-like air. A number of students were already seated when the Tangshan Tigers came in.

'Look, there are place settings,' said Olivier. 'They've split us up.'

Matt saw that the settings alternated between Beijing and Kensington students. 'That's OK,' he said. 'It'll be good to get to know some of the Kensington guys better.'

He felt a little less upbeat when he saw that his own name was placed next to that of Adam Bates. As he took his seat, he vowed that he wouldn't let Adam wind him up.

The hall filled up quickly. It was a huge, high-ceilinged, wood-panelled room, with long tables down the centre and plaques with gold writing on the walls, commemorating the achievements of pupils.

The teachers filed in – Chang Sifu and Mr Figgis were sitting with the Kensington Academy staff on the top table, on a dais at the end. Chang was next to Kawada-san, and Matt was pleased to see the grave yet friendly way they conversed together; it was obvious they held each other in high respect.

It was so different from the constant one-upmanship of people like –

'Oh no, I'm stuck next to James!' said the loud harsh voice of Adam Bates. 'What a pain!'

'Don't worry,' said Matt, keeping his cool. 'We'll get through it somehow.' After all, he reminded himself, this was his chance to get some useful information out of Adam.

Kawada-san stood and tapped on the side of a glass with a spoon. The tinkling sound echoed throughout the hall. Conversation died.

'I should like to say a few words before we eat,' said Kawada-san. He had a low, distinct voice that carried to the end of the hall. 'We are here for a tournament, which is of course a competitive occasion – but competitive in, I hope, the right spirit.'

'Yeah,' muttered Adam to Matt, 'the spirit to smash you guys!'

Matt did not respond.

'In martial arts,' said Kawada-san, 'the aim is to perfect one's own skills. We all share this goal. Martial arts teach us discipline. Respect. Skill in combat, but also peace and stillness of mind. We all share these values, I am sure. We each fight to win, pitting our skills against the very best; but at the same time, martial arts bring us closer together, teaching us respect for ourselves and for each other. I hope this tournament will bring out these values, whichever team wins.'

Matt saw Chang nodding in agreement.

Spontaneously, Matt started clapping, and in a moment the whole hall resounded to the applause. But Adam, Matt saw, gave only two or three bored, half-hearted claps.

'Chang Sifu and I are old friends and rivals,' Kawada-san resumed, 'and know something of the mutual honour and respect that performing martial arts at the highest levels can bring. And so the tournament will begin with an exhibition bout between Chang Sifu and myself.'

Wow, thought Matt. *That'll be something to see!*

'Our sensei will wipe the floor with yours!' said Adam in Matt's ear. Matt wondered if he'd understood a single word of Kawada-san's speech.

Serving staff came round with the first course of smoked salmon. Looking round the table, Matt was glad to see that most of the students were chatting away good-naturedly. He turned to the student on his other side, a slim dark-skinned boy with green eyes.

'Hi, I'm Matt.'

'Good to meet you, Matt. I'm Saeed. You're the captain, aren't you?'

'That's right. What's your martial art?'

'Judo. You?'

'Tae kwon-do.'

'Oh, a stand-up fighter? We don't have so many of those in our team. There's your friend Harry. And Shushmita, she's karate.'

Matt looked at the pretty Indian girl opposite – small and dainty but with a determined look that warned she'd be no pushover. She was talking to Carl and they seemed to be getting on very well.

'You're not related to Dan Warrick, are you?' Matt heard her say.

'Er, yeah, he's my dad.'

'I saw him in the Olympics. He is one of my heroes!'

'Yeah, well, he's pretty good at what he does.'

'And you take after him? I shall be worried if you say you do!'

'Well, y'know, I try my best,' said Carl,

blushing and grinning. *Who'd have thought Carl had a softer side?* Matt thought, smiling.

He turned back to Adam. He'd better get on with his task of trying to find out something about Adam's dad.

'That watch your dad gave you – it's awesome,' he said. 'He must be doing well.'

'That's right, James!' said Adam. 'Wanna see something good?'

'Sure, what?'

'See this?' Adam held up his mobile and showed Matt a picture of a luxury gym, with weights machines, gymnastic apparatus, a climbing wall, a huge open mat area and a swimming pool in the background. A fit-looking man in a martial arts suit stood in the centre of the mat. He had broad shoulders, a square jaw and eyebrows that almost met in the middle.

'That's my dad – and that's the new gym

we've just had installed in the basement of our house. Bet you wish your family could afford something like that!'

'Looks like it cost a lot,' said Matt.

'Oh, you bet. But that's just small change to my dad – he's a big player in the diamond trade.'

'Is that right?'

'Oh yeah. All the top people wear my dad's diamonds. There's a huge party going on tomorrow night, to celebrate the British film industry – it'll be packed with stars and most of them will be wearing Bates's diamonds.'

Matt's detective instincts kicked in. 'Where is it?' he asked casually.

'You needn't worry about that, James! It's not the sort of do they'd let *you* into.'

'I just wondered, I don't want to go –'

'That's good, 'cause you wouldn't get in!'

Matt realized he wouldn't get any more

out of Adam. Anyway, the Tangshan Tigers could find out for themselves. He turned away and struck up a conversation with Saeed about martial arts films. But his mind was buzzing. This could be just the lead the Tangshan Tigers needed.

After dinner, the Tangshan Tigers met up in the room Matt and Shawn were sharing. Matt told them what he'd learned from Adam.

'It's exactly the sort of venue where the Scorpion might strike! We just need to find out where it is – but I guess the library will be locked up now, so we won't be able to use the computers.'

'No problem,' Shawn took out his Blackberry. 'Party to celebrate British movies, right?' His fingers flew over the keypad. 'Here we are – Frobisher House in Chelsea – starts at seven thirty.'

'We should go there straight after the tournament then!' said Matt.

It was going to be a busy day tomorrow. A martial arts tournament in the afternoon. And Scorpion-hunting in the evening. Matt couldn't wait.

THE TOURNAMENT

Spectators were sitting on two sides of the combat arena. Matt recognized his mother and Mr Figgis sitting in the front row. His mother smiled and waved.

Most spectators were Kensington students, but the crowd gave a generous cheer as the Beijing squad took their places. There was another, louder cheer as Adam led out the Kensington team. The two teams were placed on opposite sides of the arena. Adam stared across at Matt. Matt met his gaze unblinkingly. *There's no way you're going to psyche me out*, he thought.

That morning, Chang had gone through the team sheet with Matt and asked him to choose the order in which the Beijing competitors should fight. Matt had asked to be matched against Adam. It was a risk, but if he didn't take this chance to face his demons, he might never get another.

Chang had inclined his head. 'Yes. It is right that, as captain, you take on the hardest task for yourself.'

Very soon, Matt would know the outcome.

Before the tournament proper began, though, there was the exhibition match between Chang Sifu and Kawada-san. Matt led the applause of his team as the two martial arts masters met on the *tatami* and bowed.

The bout began with Chang going on the attack, demonstrating the techniques of kung fu – high kicks, whirling kicks, sweep kicks, spear-hand strikes from a distance and close-range, dazzling combinations of kicks and punches. Kawada-san blocked, evaded, countered. Matt held his breath; the skill of both men was dazzling. The speed of the moves was incredible. There was a slight difference in their styles: Kawada-san seemed more explosive, while Chang seemed to move with a more fluid grace. In terms of skill, though, there was little to choose between them.

Chang had the edge in the first part of the bout. But after that they moved on to an exhibition of ju-jitsu skills. Kawada-san threw Chang repeatedly; and got him in holds, which Chang would wriggle out of, only to get held again. It was only an exhibition bout, Matt told himself – Chang was graciously letting Kawada-san demonstrate his techniques.

Yet it made Matt uneasy. Kawada-san was hot stuff and Chang clearly respected him.

'Whoa!' said Shawn. 'They know how to do it, those two! Wonder if we'll ever fight as well as that?'

'Maybe,' said Matt. 'One day.'

'He's good, Kawada-san,' said Olivier. 'As good as Chang.'

'Well, almost.' said Catarina.

'And that probably means his team are pretty hot too,' said Shawn.

'They're going to be the toughest opponents we've ever faced,' said Matt seriously.

The exhibition bout ended and the two masters bowed to each other. The crowd applauded.

It was time for the tournament to begin.

Five–two. To Kensington.

The bouts had contained a few surprises.

Andrei and Jahmal (whom Matt hadn't regarded as his strongest fighters) both won for Beijing. Abdul had lost to Harry Vincent-Bennett. Lola and Paolo had also lost. So had Olivier – he'd fought heroically against Saeed, a ju-jitsu exponent, who'd drawn him into a close-quarters fight, which wasn't his style. Use of the *Chi Sao* technique had kept him in it and he'd avoided being caught in a hold – but the judges gave it on points to Kensington.

Matt had matched Carl against Shushmita, reasoning that Carl would use his karate skills best against another *karateka*. With Carl's advantage in weight and reach he'd expected him to win – but Shushmita was very quick and got under Carl's guard to strike repeatedly and win on points.

'Bad luck,' Matt said to Carl after the bout – rather cautiously, hoping that Carl wouldn't explode in a temper. To his surprise, Carl took defeat well. He gave a crooked smile.

'It happens,' he said. 'She's good.'

Over halfway through, and three down. The Beijing team had it all to do.

'We can still do it,' Matt told his team. 'If we win the rest . . .'

'Course we'll do it!' said Catarina.

'It's up to you, Wolfgang,' said Matt. 'You can even the score here.'

'*Ja*,' said Wolfgang. He moistened his lips nervously.

'Remember *Chi Sao*,' said Chang quietly.

Wolfgang's opponent was a ju-jitsu specialist. He went straight for Wolfgang and very nearly threw him in the first minute – but Wolfgang remembered the counter-move Matt had used yesterday, to roll with the throw and then shift balance at the last moment. His opponent hit the mat, but managed to pull Wolfgang with him. It wasn't a pretty fight — a lot of tussling and wriggling on the floor. But finally Wolfgang got the Kensington fighter in a choke-hold from which he couldn't free himself, and at last submitted. The judges awarded the bout to Wolfgang.

Five—three.

It was Matt's turn.

Time seemed to slow down as he walked out to the centre. The crowd were shouting and cheering, but he was hardly aware of the noise. He breathed deeply, willing himself to relax — you couldn't fight at your best if you felt tense, he knew.

Adam's chin tilted upwards aggressively; he stared at Matt through heavy-lidded eyes.

'I'm going to squash you like a bug, James. Just like I used to do in the playground.'

'We'll see about that,' said Matt quietly. He bowed.

The fight began.

Keep him at a distance, Matt said to himself. He knew he had the weapons to score points off Adam and win, as long as Adam didn't draw him into a close-range fight.

He concentrated on the centre line technique, getting his balance right and starting off with two great punches with his full weight behind them. Adam blocked with his hands, but was taken aback by the speed and power of Matt's attack. He was retreating before Matt's onslaught.

Matt got in a high thrusting kick that caught Adam in the chest and made him give ground still further.

The Beijing team roared their support.

I can do this, thought Matt. *I've got him!*

He pressed forward with a combination of punches – but Adam evaded them, plunged in and grabbed Matt by the waist. The next instant Matt found himself lifted clear off the ground. He felt Adam's thick strong arms squeezing him – he could hardly breathe.

Now it was the turn of the Kensington supporters to roar.

Matt struggled, but his feet couldn't find the floor, he had nothing to push against.

Adam slammed Matt down on the floor and fell on top, trying to pin him down. One of his hands pressed Matt's arm to the floor. Matt could still barely breathe, and his wrist-bone hurt where Adam was forcing it down. But worse than the pain was the thought that he could lose this – the advantage gained by his early kick must be cancelled out now.

If Adam pinned the other arm, the hold would be complete.

Defeat stared Matt in the face.

Remember Chi Sao . . .

Conscious of Adam's heavy body lying across his, Matt *felt* what was happening. Before Adam could grab his other hand to complete the pin, Matt had moved it. As Adam shifted his weight to try and restrict the movement of Matt's free arm, Matt instinctively rolled *his* weight in the opposite direction.

For a split second he was free of Adam's crushing weight. Before Adam could adjust, Matt made an explosive effort and wriggled free. He felt Adam clutch at his arm, but too late. Matt bounced to his feet. *Yes!* he thought. *I'm free!*

The roars of the Beijing supporters rang in his ears.

Adam's face distorted with rage. He rushed at Matt, his head low, trying to repeat the manoeuvre of lifting Matt up by the waist.

But Matt was ready for that now. He

checked Adam's rush with a double-handed block and threw a short straight punch right through the centre line, which hit Adam in the midriff. Choking for breath, Adam backed off.

But Adam was strong. He recovered from the blow fast. He circled Matt warily, looking for another chance to get in close.

Another rush – again, Matt blocked and counter-attacked, scoring with another strike to the body.

The buzzer went for the end of the bout.

The two fighters stood panting, waiting for the verdict.

Have I done enough to win? Matt wondered.

The judges consulted briefly.

'The winner is . . . Matt James!' announced the head judge.

A wave of relief flooded through Matt. The Beijing team went wild. There was applause from some of the Kensington side too.

'What?' shouted Adam. 'No way! I had him down; it's not fair, I pinned him!'

An embarrassed silence filled the auditorium. Harry Vincent-Bennett came forward and said quietly: 'Leave it, Adam. You have to accept the judges' decision; don't show the team up.'

'But I should have won!'

Kawada-san walked on to the *tatami*. He touched Adam on the shoulder. 'Enough,' he said. 'You were fairly beaten.'

'What? I had him down, it's not fair!'

'The hold was not good,' said Kawada-san. 'If you cannot accept defeat with dignity, you are not fit to be captain.'

As Adam stomped back to his place, Matt saw tears glistening in his eyes.

'That was fantastic, Matt!' said Olivier, clapping him on the back.

'It's still four–five to them, though,' said Matt. 'We have to win the next two! Shawn – are you up for it?'

Shawn grinned. 'You know I am!'

Shawn's opponent was a ju-jitsu specialist. They grappled furiously, striving for advantage. After a long tense struggle, Shawn's opponent got him in a choke-hold – but before he could tighten the hold, Shawn wriggled free, twisted his opponent round and applied an armlock. He forced the Kensington fighter to the mat and held on.

The buzzer went.

Five–five!

The noise was indescribable now.

'Go, Catarina!' said Matt.

'I'll see what I can do,' said Catarina.

Catarina's opponent was another judo exponent. He followed the usual Kensington technique of trying to get in close and grapple and take her down – but Catarina simply didn't let him. She danced just out of reach, launching kicks at head-level, picking him off with long-range blows. It was like watching a graceful matador against a charging bull. Matt's voice was hoarse with cheering. The Kensington fighter tried gamely until the very end, but he never broke through Catarina's defence.

The buzzer went for the final time.

Six–five to Beijing!

Chang Sifu was on his feet, clapping. So were Matt's mum and Mr Figgis.

And so was Kawada-san.

Matt grinned at his tired but triumphant team. 'Well done, you guys! We've broken Kensington's winning streak!'

And I beat Adam Bates, he thought to himself.

'Yeah, well done,' said Harry, coming over
to congratulate them. 'Well done, Matt.'

'Thanks,' said Matt. 'It was close! You're
taking it pretty well.'

'Not much else I can do, is there?' said
Harry, smiling resignedly. 'Anyway, there's
some consolation – Kawada-san just told me
he's making me the new captain! Hey, listen,
have you heard about the outing tonight?
Don't know where we're going – Kawada-san
says it's a surprise; are you coming?'

'Er, dunno,' said Matt. Chang Sifu had not
mentioned any outing to him. 'Maybe, if it's
a bit later on. There's something we've got to
do first.'

'What's that?' asked Harry.

Matt glanced at the other Tangshan Tigers.
'Oh, there's this party we thought we'd drop
into.'

LEAP IN THE DARK

They slipped out of a side-door. It was nearly dark, the street-lights a hazy yellow, the moon a silver crescent against the sky's deep velvety blue. As they walked away from the Academy Matt glanced back and thought he saw the silhouette of someone standing at the window. Was that Chang Sifu? The figure gave a nod of approval.

'This way,' said Matt, leading the Tigers down the street.

'You memorized the route from the map, did you?' asked Shawn.

'No need – I used to live in London, remember?'

Matt led them quickly through a succession of streets and squares and along Chelsea Embankment. Lights twinkled in the dark water of the Thames. Chelsea Bridge was lit up like a fairground ride.

'It's this way,' said Matt. They crossed the road, dodging taxis, and found themselves in a square of stately white mansions. Frobisher House was the largest and grandest. Bright lights shone from the windows; two uniformed doormen in top hats stood outside and limousines were parked bumper to bumper.

'Now we've just got to get in,' said Matt. 'Olivier – any ideas?'

'I'll see if I can blag us in.' Olivier could usually charm his way through any situation. He went up the steps and approached the doormen.

'Excuse me,' he began – but that was as far as he got.

There was a crash. Shouts, screams, gasps of terror. Fragments of glass showered on to the pavement, making the Tigers jump back.

'Hey, what was that?' shouted Catarina.

The masked, black-clad figure of the Scorpion had smashed through an upper-storey window and landed in the branches of a plane tree. A diamond necklace glittered in his hand. As Matt watched, he thrust the necklace into a backpack, then swarmed down the tree, hit the ground running and was off down a side road.

'Let's go!' said Matt. The Scorpion was fast

and agile — but he wasn't going to be a match for four Tangshan Tigers!

They pelted round the corner and stopped in bewilderment. An empty road stretched ahead.

'But how —' said Matt.

'Look!' said Catarina.

The Scorpion was halfway up the wall of a house. He was climbing fast, making use of drainpipes, window sills and projecting masonry.

'So that's how he does it,' said Shawn. 'That's why no one ever sees where he goes!'

'It's called *le parkour*,' said Olivier. 'An extreme urban climbing sport — I've seen it done in Paris. And this guy's good.'

'So what do we do?' asked Shawn. 'Call the cops?'

'Unless Catarina's got a better idea . . .' said Matt.

'Aye aye, Captain!' said Catarina. She launched herself at the wall, grabbed a drainpipe and shot up it like a squirrel.

High above, the Scorpion was hauling himself up on to the roof. He disappeared from sight. Matt held his breath as Catarina followed. He hoped the Scorpion hadn't seen her – if he had, it would be easy to push her off as she clambered on to the roof.

But Catarina reached the top, looked down and gave a thumbs-up. She pointed in the direction the Scorpion had gone; then she disappeared from view.

'Come on!' said Matt. They sprinted in the direction Catarina had indicated. As they came into the next street Matt saw the Scorpion, like a black bat against the dark blue sky. He jumped across a gap from one roof to another.

Matt's guts tingled. The gap was no more than two metres, but the drop was more like twenty. If Catarina miscalculated . . .

Her long agile figure flew across the gap and landed safely. Matt breathed again.

Once more, Catarina pointed in the direction she was going.

'She can't call down to us,' Matt whispered to the others. 'Otherwise the Scorpion will hear. We'll have to keep up and watch what she does!'

They pounded down the next street. Matt saw the Scorpion jump and land with a roll on to a lower flat roof. From where they were they could see him clearly. He stood, looking around, perhaps he was planning his next jump – or perhaps he had heard Catarina's footsteps behind him? Catarina had not yet come into view.

Matt thought quickly. He stooped and picked up a stone. He tossed it up on the roof. It landed with a sharp clatter near the Scorpion, who spun round.

Catarina appeared on the opposite roof. The three Tigers on the ground frantically gestured at her. Catarina saw, and dodged behind a chimney stack, just before the Scorpion turned round again. For a long moment, he stood as if in thought.

Then he set off running again and leapt on to the next roof.

Catarina followed.

The Tigers kept up as best they could. It was hard going – they had to run twice as far as Catarina, running the whole length of streets when she only had to jump from one block to another.

They rounded another corner and saw something that made Matt's blood run cold.

The Scorpion leapt across the whole width of the street — a huge leap, it had to be at least five metres.

Don't do it! Matt tried to send a telepathic message to Catarina. *It's better to let the Scorpion escape than kill yourself . . .*

Catarina came to the edge of the roof and without a pause hurled herself into the void.

Matt saw her, outlined against the sky.

He saw her lose height, saw her fling her arms out desperately —

saw her fingertips grasp the roof edge —

felt the shock as her knees thudded into the wall —

saw her legs scrabble until they found a ledge where she could rest her weight —

and sighed with relief as she pulled herself up to safety.

'Phew!' said Shawn shakily.

'Go, Catarina,' said Olivier.

They ran in the direction the Scorpion had been heading.

But there was no sign of him. The rooftops were empty. A couple of evening strollers, seeing Matt and the Tigers desperately scanning the sky, looked up too. But there was nothing to see.

'We've lost him,' said Matt heavily. 'I don't know what to do next. You don't think he could have seen her . . .?'

Matt jumped as his mobile went off.

'Yes?'

'It's Catarina. He is climbing down – Endicott Street, you know it?'

'Yeah, I know it. Near the Embankment,' replied Matt.

'Meet you down on the ground then!' Catarina's voice was faint.

'Hey, Catarina?'

'Yeah?'

'You were awesome!'

The Scorpion marched briskly towards the river. They saw him pull off his mask, stuff it in his pocket and put on a baseball cap.

'Bit less conspicuous,' said Olivier. 'He must be going where there'll be people around.'

'Keep close,' said Matt softly. 'Be ready to make a move.'

The Scorpion went through a small gap in the wall and descended a flight of steps carved into the embankment, leading down to the river.

'This is it,' said Matt. 'Let's go!'

They ran to the wall and peered down. The Scorpion was just jumping into a speedboat – a big, beautiful, blue and silver speedboat. There was a pile of boxes in the back, and at the front a small wheelhouse.

The Scorpion untied the rope that moored it to the wall, and sat down at the wheel.

He gunned the engine into life.

'Now!' said Matt.

He leapt over the wall, ran down the first few steps and jumped into the back of the speedboat. The other Tigers landed almost simultaneously. The boat rocked, but the water was choppy anyway with the waves created by passing craft, and the noise was covered by the roar of the engine. The Scorpion didn't turn round.

They crouched behind the boxes as the boat powered out into the middle of the river and set off.

'Now what?' asked Olivier.

'We watch,' said Matt. 'And we see what he does with the diamonds.'

★

The boat did not travel very far. After
five minutes, it passed under Westminster
Bridge, with the Houses of Parliament
glowing yellow against the evening sky,
and crossed the river to dock on the south
side.

The Scorpion tied up the boat and leapt
nimbly up the steps.

'Leave it a minute, just in case he looks
round,' said Matt, holding up a restraining
hand. 'OK, that should do it.'

Cautiously, they emerged on to the South
Bank. The Scorpion was striding along,
dodging through the crowds of tourists who
were on their way to concerts and
restaurants, or simply taking an evening stroll
to admire the view. The backpack swung on
his shoulder.

Matt stepped up the pace; it wouldn't
matter if the Scorpion saw them now – he

would think they were part of the crowd. Matt hoped to get a glimpse of his face, but the baseball cap kept it in shadow.

'Looks like he's heading for the London Eye,' said Matt.

The colossal white wheel towered above them, each spoke the length of a giant redwood. As he neared the queue that snaked away from the Eye, the Scorpion slowed down. He greeted two men in dark suits. They exchanged a few words, but the Tigers weren't near enough to catch what they said. The Scorpion patted his backpack.

'Those guys must be his buyers,' said Shawn. 'They're going to take the diamonds off his hands.'

'Yes,' breathed Matt, 'on the London Eye. You can book a pod to yourself – you couldn't get a much more private place for selling stolen diamonds. They'll be over a hundred metres in the air – who's going to see anything?'

'I am!' said Catarina.

'What? How are you going to get in the pod without being noticed?' asked Matt.

'I'm not gonna get in the pod! I'm gonna climb up outside – take a picture of that Scorpion through the glass with my mobile when they hand over the diamonds! Then we can give the evidence to the cops and the cops can bust them good!'

'If you're taking pictures,' said Shawn, 'use this.' He handed her a miniature digital camera. 'Better than a mobile – sharper definition.'

'But it's too dangerous!' protested Matt. 'I mean, look at the size of it – look how high it is!'

'Doesn't matter how high it is, if you don't fall!' said Catarina. 'And I ain't gonna fall!'

'If anyone can do it, Catarina can,' said Olivier.

'Anyway, there's not much time!' said Catarina. 'Look, they're getting into their pod now.'

'OK, Catarina, do it,' said Matt. 'But be careful!'

Matt didn't expect a reply. Catarina was already running through the crowds towards the London Eye.

SKY HIGH

Catarina stopped by the side of the South Bank wall, only a few metres from the barrier, gazing up at the huge, slowly turning wheel. Two uniformed security staff, a man and a woman, were taking people's tickets and letting them on, filling one pod at a time. Matt saw the dilemma: if she climbed over the barrier in plain view, the guards would stop her.

'We'd better help,' said Olivier. 'We have to create a diversion.'

'Like what?' said Matt.

'We'll think of something. Come on!'

The Tigers ran to the foot of the Eye, where the slow-moving queue ascended a ramp that led to the pods. They threaded their way through the queue, ignoring the angry looks of those waiting in line. The guards stopped them.

'Tickets, please!'

'Oh, wait a minute!' said Olivier. 'I'm sure I had the tickets somewhere, or did I leave them in my other jacket? I'm so sorry!'

A family with three children at the front of the line began to protest.

'No, we're definitely next,' Olivier assured them. 'We were before you, you just didn't see us.'

The man turned to his wife and said something in German. Olivier, who was fluent in German, quickly addressed him in the same language, smiling politely. The man looked bewildered.

'What's going on?' said the male guard. 'What's all this about?'

'We're getting on, that's what,' said Shawn, and ran towards the nearest pod.

'Oh no, you don't!' said the guard.

'Oh yes, we do!' said Oliver, dodging round him. The other guard quickly blocked his way.

'Come on, you've got to let us on – all these people have pushed in front of us!' said Matt.

Out of the corner of his eye, he saw Catarina nimbly vault over the barrier and run towards the base of the wheel.

She leapt on to one of the slowly revolving spokes and began to shimmy her way up it.

The crowd behind the Tigers were getting restless.

'You're not getting on without tickets!' said the female guard.

'Oh, sorry!' said Olivier. 'My mistake, I've just remembered our tickets are for tomorrow! I'm so sorry, what a foolish mistake, I must apologize if we've caused any delay.' He apologized handsomely in German to the family.

'Clear off out of it then!' said the male guard irritably.

A gasp went up from the crowd. People pointed up at what the Tigers already knew was happening – high above, Catarina was swinging her way from bar to bar, as agile as a gibbon. Already she was a third of the way up.

The two guards looked at one another in panic. 'What do we do? Can we get it stopped?' said the woman guard.

'But then everyone will be stuck up there in the pods!'

'Better report it —'

'Don't let anyone else on —'

Matt and the Tigers retreated to the walkway and watched as Catarina climbed higher and higher. A crowd was gathering on the South Bank.

'Must be some kind of stunt!' he heard someone say.

'But where are the TV cameras?' asked someone else.

Matt froze as he saw Catarina grab for a strut and miss.

As she fell, she twisted in mid-air and grabbed another. She resumed her climb as if nothing had happened.

'I can't bear to watch,' said Olivier.

'If she falls from there, she's a goner!' said Shawn. Catarina was now almost at the very top of the Eye. She appeared no larger than a speck.

'She'd be all right if she fell in the water,' said Matt hopefully.

'She wouldn't,' said Shawn. 'From that height, it'd be like hitting concrete.'

Catarina was directly above the Scorpion's pod now. Matt saw her hang on with one hand while she snapped photos with the other.

She started to climb down fast, taking the most direct route via the centre of the wheel.

Matt breathed out. It looked like she'd made it. Every stage in the descent brought her closer to safety.

The Scorpion's pod was swinging downwards too. Matt had the odd sense that it was pursuing Catarina. And in a way, it was. Matt saw the Scorpion and the two dark-suited men pointing at her. As the pod swung nearer he saw their faces were tense and angry.

Catarina had been rumbled.

She reached the bottom and somersaulted over the barrier. Eluding the security staff who tried to grab her, she ran down the ramp and joined the Tigers.

'Catarina!' said Matt, clutching her shoulders. 'You nearly gave me a heart attack – but you did it!'

'Yup,' said Catarina, grinning. She held up the digital camera. 'Got the goods!'

'And someone's going to get us if we don't watch out!' said Shawn. 'Look!'

The Scorpion and his two buyers were striding purposefully towards them, cutting their way through the crowd.

'Let's just get out of here and find the nearest police station,' said Olivier. 'We've got what we came for.'

'Wait,' said Matt. 'We need to see what this Scorpion guy looks like.'

If his face didn't come out clearly in Catarina's picture, they had no description to give the police. The whole evening's work would have been wasted.

It was risky. The Scorpion was on his way and he was dangerous – Matt knew he was fast and agile enough to attack and still get away, even in this crowd.

But he had to see the man who'd attacked and robbed his mother.

His heart beat fast as he stopped, turned and faced the three men.

The Scorpion's baseball cap was tilted back.

At last, Matt got a clear view of his face.

It was Frank Bates.

Frank Bates? Matt's mind was in a whirl. Why would Bates be stealing his own diamonds?

But there was no doubt about it. The man had the same broad shoulders, square jaw and extended eyebrows Matt had seen in the picture on Adam's mobile. Now he understood why Bates needed a private gym with a climbing wall – the man had to be super-fit to do what he did.

Bates held out his hand. 'Give me that camera,' he said to Catarina.

'I don't think so,' said Catarina.

'Then let me see if I can make you think differently,' said Bates. His voice was cold, hard and confident – the voice of a man accustomed to getting his own way.

He moved purposefully towards Catarina. She held up the camera tantalizingly, then lightly tossed it over Bates's head to Matt. Matt was taken by surprise but caught it neatly.

Bates took a step towards Matt. Matt threw the camera to Olivier, who plucked it out of the air one-handed.

'I'm not playing games!' said Bates through gritted teeth.

'Aren't you?' said Olivier, tossing the camera to Shawn.

A crowd had formed in a loose ring around them, as passers-by stepped aside to give them room, then stopped to see what was going on. That section of the South Bank walkway was full of street performers – every few metres there were jugglers, living statues, stilt-walkers and musicians. The crowd obviously assumed that the Tangshan Tigers were another act. They stood and applauded at the deft display of catching.

Bates's buyers had melted away. They'd got what they came for. Bates, on the other hand, was trapped, Matt realized. He would probably have loved to melt away too, instead of being gawped at by tourists, but he couldn't afford to leave the incriminating evidence on the camera behind.

'I don't want to hurt you kids,' he hissed. 'But I will if you don't hand that over. Don't mess me with me – I'm a ju-jitsu expert!'

'Come and get it!' said Shawn, and as Bates rushed at him he threw the camera back to Catarina.

But this time Bates changed his tactics. He went straight for Shawn and knocked him off his feet. He pushed Shawn face-down on the ground and got him in an armlock. Matt saw by the practised way he moved that Bates was skilled as well as strong and fit.

'Now hand over the camera! Or I'll snap his arm like a twig!'

The crowd of tourists gasped in mock-horror.

Catarina came towards Bates, holding out the camera. As Bates reached for it, Shawn rolled over, releasing the pressure of Bates's hold; at the same time, Catarina pulled the camera back so that Bates's fingers closed on empty air.

Too bad for him he doesn't know Chi Sao! thought Matt.

Shawn jumped to his feet. The crowd clapped and cheered.

'Right,' said Bates. 'You kids have asked for it!'

He ran at Catarina. She kicked out, but Bates brushed the kick aside, grabbed her, and got her in a choke-hold. But Catarina had anticipated and got her arm through to prevent the hold squeezing her neck. Olivier came in and dealt Bates a kung-fu kick in the ribs that made him grunt. Catarina danced free.

Again the crowd applauded.

Bates turned like a baited bear and went

for Olivier. Matt stepped in between them and hit Bates with a combination of two spear-hand strikes, right down the centre line. Bates growled and backed off; Matt went in for another strike, but Bates read this one and grabbed Matt's hand. Before he could turn and twist in the classic ju-jitsu move, however, Shawn wrestled his arm away and turned to throw him – but Bates saw that one coming and yanked Shawn backwards. Before he could strike or get Shawn in a hold, Catarina came in and forced him off with a flurry of high kicks.

Massive applause from the crowd!

'They're good, aren't they?' said someone.

Bates was a skilled fighter and immensely strong. He could easily have dealt with any one of the Tangshan Tigers, no doubt – but all four of them were too much for him to handle. Each time the Tigers fought him off, the crowd roared its approval. This seemed to madden Bates. His attacks became desperate.

Matt blocked a punch aimed at his face; Shawn caught Bates's arm and wrenched it downwards; Olivier caught the other arm and did the same, as Catarina swept Bates's legs from under him.

Bates slowly collapsed like a detonated tower block.

Matt, Olivier and Shawn held him face-down on the ground.

Catarina ironically bowed to the crowd.

A tinkling shower of coins landed around the Tangshan Tigers.

'Stand aside, please!'

Four police officers pushed through the crowd. The leader, a sergeant in a peaked cap, stood before the Tangshan Tigers with his hands on his hips.

'What's all this then?'

'We caught the Scorpion for you – there he is!' said Catarina, pointing to the struggling figure on the ground. She held out Shawn's digital camera. 'And all the evidence you need's in here!'

'That's another successful case for the Tangshan Tigers,' said Matt, as he watched the police lead the glowering Bates away.

'Tigers rule!' said Catarina.

'But what I don't get,' said Matt, 'is why he was stealing his own diamonds.'

'That's easy,' said Olivier. 'They were insured. Every time they got stolen, he claimed on the insurance – probably for more than their value. Not only that, he could sell them on the black market too, and get paid twice over!'

'Clever,' admitted Matt.

'Not as clever as the Tangshan Tigers, though!' said Shawn.

Matt felt more than the usual satisfaction at solving a case. This one had been personal. The Scorpion had attacked and frightened his mother. Now the Scorpion was behind bars, and it was Matt and the Tigers who'd put him there.

Matt heard a gentle cough behind him.

He spun round.

There stood Chang Sifu. He'd changed out of his martial arts suit and was wearing his favourite kingfisher blue jacket.

'You have had busy evening – quite finished now?'

'Er – yes. Quite finished, thanks, Sifu!'

'Good – then perhaps you would care to join us for evening outing?'

He pointed a hand at the London Eye. Matt saw that it was taking passengers on again, and standing in line were the two teams of Beijing and Kensington.

'But how did you know we'd be here?' asked Matt in confusion.

'I did not know. You left before I could inform you of tonight's outing. A pure coincidence that you are here!'

'A lucky one!' said Shawn.

'Yes. Now let us board, before rest of team goes without us!'

They joined their team in the queue just before a pod became available. Matt and the Tigers kept their heads down as they passed the security staff, ignoring the disapproving looks they received.

Chang Sifu and the Beijing team had one pod to themselves; Kawada-san and the Kensington team took the next.

Harry caught Matt's eye and waved. He waved back.

The ascent of the pod was so smooth Matt was surprised to find himself already several metres high and rising. The Thames fell away below, the buildings slowly assuming doll's-house proportions.

'This is a more comfortable way to get to the top, you can take my word on that!' whispered Catarina.

The Tigers laughed. 'I bet it is!' said Shawn.

Matt glanced over at Chang Sifu, who was sitting quietly on the bench at the end, taking in the spectacular sight of the illuminated London skyline. As if suddenly conscious of Matt's gaze, he turned.

Chang didn't exactly smile, but was that a twitch of the lips? Did Chang really have no idea that the Tigers would be here, hunting down the Scorpion? Or did he know much more than he was letting on? Who could tell? All Matt knew was, he was happy to be here with his friends, having foiled the Scorpion, looking out over London. His home town. But he realized that Beijing had also become his home. And it would be good to get back.

There were sure to be more adventures waiting for him and his friends. And he knew the Tangshan Tigers would be ready – whatever was thrown at them.

Masters of Martial Arts
Fighters of Crime
together they're the

TANGSHAN TIGERS

Matt

Shawn

Tangshan Tigers: The Golden Key

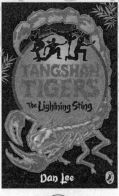

Tangshan Tigers: The Stolen Jade — Dan Lee

Tangshan Tigers: The Invisible Cloud

Tangshan Tigers: The Silent Enemy — Dan Lee

Tangshan Tigers: The Lightning Sting — Dan Lee

Tangshan Tigers: The Silver Shadow — Dan Lee

Catarina

puffin.co.uk

Olivier

TANGSHAN TIGERS

Olivier Girard

Age: 12

Nationality: Swiss

Sport: Kung fu

Special skill: Speaks three languages

Strengths: The son of a Swiss diplomat, Olivier can talk his way out of any situation. The group can always rely on him for undercover missions because of his confidence and charm.

Weaknesses: Sometimes he talks his way right into trouble!

Join the Team and Win a Prize!

Do YOU have what it takes to be a Tangshan Tiger?

Answer the questions below for the chance to win an exclusive Tangshan Tigers kit bag. Kit bag contains T-shirt, headband and cloth badge.*

1. What is the Chinese term for 'training hall'?
   a) *Kwoon*   **b)** *Karateka*   **c)** *Kufu*

2. Catarina's specialty is capoeira. Which country does this martial art come from?
   a) Britain   **b)** Bolivia   **c)** Brazil

3. In Karate, a sequence of movements performed without a partner is called *kata*.
   a) True   **b)** False

Send your answers in to us with your name, date of birth and address. Each month we will put every correct answer in a draw and pick out one lucky winner.

Tangshan Tigers Competition, Puffin Marketing, 80 Strand, London WC2R 0RL

Closing date is 31 August 2010.

Open to UK residents aged 6 or over. If you are under 13 you will need to include written permission from your parent or guardian

*subject to change